# Isabella's Libretto

Published in the United States of America
by
Excalibur Press
P. O. Box 8797
Mobile, Alabama 36689
Excaliburpress@msn.com
www.excaliburpress.us


Cover Design and Illustration by Hannah Wilson
www.hbproductions.net


Printed in the United States of America
First Edition, 2014
ISBN 978-0-9820629-2-0

# Teen Readers Say

*Isabella's Libretto* is a classic tale of everlasting love between a mother and daughter and of friendship between two orphan girls, Isabella and Catherine. Both girls are in Antonio Vivaldi's Orchestra at *Ospedale della Pietà*, one of the city's orphanages. I liked the way the writer took us back in time, nearly three hundred years, but the girls in 1715 connect with girls today. My mom and I read the book together and we enjoyed it.

> Ashley Wade, 14-year-old poet
> Spartanburg, South Carolina

Isabella is a proud, strong-willed teenager. When these traits get her in trouble, she learns that helping the new young orphan learn to play the cello isn't the worst punishment one could be dealt. Through the story, Monica, Isabella, and her friend Catherine go through the tears of sorrow and jubilance of new opportunities.

> Joely Crawford, 13-year-old violinist
> Amarillo, Texas

*Isabella's Libretto* is a beautifully written story that will capture your heart...the kind of book that you stay up too late reading!

> Charlotte York, 12-year-old oboist
> Nashville, Tennessee

If you would like to share your comments on *Isabella's Libretto* with other readers, submit them (with contact information) to:

Excalibur Press, P.O. Box 8797, Mobile, Alabama 36689.

Or post comments on our blog at www.excaliburpress.us

Or at the Author's website: www.kimteter.com

After all, teen readers rule.

For my mother,

Mary Joyce Koehler Cross


And her mother,

Cecilia Elizabeth Peysen Koehler

# Isabella's Libretto

### A Novel

### Kimberly Cross Teter

**Excalibur Press 2014**

**Mobile, Alabama**

*Venice, Italy  1715*

# A Brief Historical Note

In the early part of the eighteenth century, travelers from all over Europe flocked to Venice, Italy, to hear the brilliant orchestra at the *Ospedale della Pietà* — an orchestra that was comprised entirely of females. Most of the girls in the orchestra were abandoned as babies at the *Ospedale*, one of Venice's four homes for the city's neediest inhabitants. Instead of being treated as cast-offs of society, the girls were sheltered and educated in the *Pietà*, where life was closely tied to Catholic observances. Antonio Vivaldi, famed music composer and violinist, worked off and on for the *Pietà* from 1703 until 1740. He taught there, directed the celebrated orchestra, and wrote hundreds of pieces that were performed by the girls.

The *Ospedale della Pietà* provided a home to thousands of children over the span of several centuries and, in fact, still operates today as an early childhood education center. What follows is a fictional tale about one of the girls, Isabella dal Cello, who *might* have lived there in the year 1715.

**(More historical observations can be found at the close of this novel under *Author's Note*.)**

# Isabella's Libretto

*Venice, Italy*
*5 March 1715*

## Chapter One
### *The New Girl*

Will my best friend forgive me if I can find the right words to apologize? I am haunted once again by this question now that Don Vivaldi has dismissed us from practice and I no longer need to give all my attention to my cello.

I made her so angry, so very angry. "Isabella dal Cello, what is it you want?" Catherine spoke these words to me—no!—she hurled these words at me that night in the chapel after we got into so much trouble. And she has not spoken one word to me since.

Well, I know what I want—I want Don Antonio Vivaldi to write a cello concerto that features me. I want to be the girl with the red pomegranate blossom in her hair who goes to the front of the orchestra and plays for all of Venice. I want to be the girl that the audience adores.

But tonight? Tonight I just want my best friend back. I want Catherine to sit with me at supper, and I want Catherine to braid my hair in the morning, and then I will braid hers. When rehearsal is over and our music put away, I want to link my arm in hers and go down the stairs whispering secrets. Because that is what we used to do before we had our fight ten–no, eleven days ago.

Now that rehearsal is over and the other girls are drifting away, I have my chance. I want to apologize. I pause as I wipe down the strings of my cello, and I look across the hall at Catherine. She is putting her music in order, but she must feel my eyes. Ah, she looks up at me...but now she looks back down at her oboe and will not meet my gaze. I take a deep breath and once again practice the words that might make everything right.

I still don't understand how Catherine can be so certain she has a mother somewhere when there is so much I don't know. Someone abandoned me here at the *Ospedale della Pietà* when I was just a baby, so I don't know who my mother is...or was. I don't even know if my real name is Isabella dal Cello, so it's hard for me to understand Catherine's feelings. I want so badly to make up with her that I will cross the room to meet Catherine on her side. She is the only one remaining now in her area of the music hall.

She ignores me as I step toward her.

"Catherine," I say, "please look at me." Slowly she raises her head and studies me as I continue. "I am truly sorry for the things I said to you that night." My heart beats faster with her silence. At last she speaks.

"Isabella, you were very mean to me." Her blue eyes pierce me with accusation. "Very mean."

"But I am not mean," I protest. "I truly, truly am not mean. I was tired and I was scared and I called you a name that I know you hate. But I am not mean."

2

She turns her gaze to the tall window, and my eyes follow as my fingers fidget with the embroidered edge on my apron. Outside, beyond the walls of our orphanage, long shadows of winter's late afternoon creep across the waters of the lagoon. A few seagulls dip and glide close to the black gondolas crossing the wide mouth of the canal.

"Please, Catherine, I said I was sorry. I know you cannot stay mad for long." She doesn't disguise a shadow of a smile as she looks directly into my eyes.

"It has been eleven days," I add.

"Let me think about it," she says, pushing a stray wisp of blonde hair from her forehead. Slowly she stands, a hint of forgiveness shimmering in her eyes. "You are right. I never could stay mad at you for long, so I think I will accept your apology." Her mouth forms a half smile, but her voice is firm. "But I ask you to remember always that I am Catherine—not *Caterina*—and that I am English. It is who I am."

Catherine has never been able to hold a grudge. I bite my tongue because I am relieved to see the flash of merriment once again in her blue eyes, joy that has been missing since that night we got into so much trouble with Signora Priora. Yes, if the price of our friendship is my acceptance of her childish belief that her mother will come back to get her, then so be it.

"Do you promise?" she asks.

I nod. "I agree," I say with a grin. I hum a five-note musical phrase in a minor key. She beams and hums her response, the rest of the melody we composed together. I have missed our secret song, and now I'm relieved that we are best friends again.

"We can sit together later at supper," I say.

At that moment the gong of the bell reverberates throughout the music room and tolls the hour, calling us to evening prayers.

3

With satisfaction, I retreat to pack up my instrument, and as I do so, Annamaria rushes past on her way to the chapel downstairs. She is the best violinist and, I think, Don Vivaldi's favorite of us all.

"We need to go," Catherine calls, glancing around the near-empty room, "or we'll be late to vespers. Hurry! It always takes you a long time to put away your cello."

"Her name is Speranza," I say. "My cello is named Speranza…"

Before I can continue, a discordant run of loud thuds coming from below startles me.

*Thwack! Thwack! Thwack!*

"Is that the front door?" I look over my shoulder. "That's strange. Nobody should be at the front door this time of evening." I lay Speranza gently on her side and turn toward the doorway. And again, even louder — *Thwack! Thwack! Thwack!*

"I wonder who it is."

"We don't have time," pleads Catherine. "I don't want to get in trouble again."

"Oh, but I want to look. Just a quick look." The massive double door opening onto the *fondamenta*, the wide walkway adjacent to the Grand Canal, is hardly used except for special events here at the *Pietà*.

Catherine heaves a sigh, holds her oboe close to her chest, and tip-toes behind me into the hallway. We kneel and peer through the stairwell banister to the foyer three floors below. Even though we are high above, we see Signora Priora stride from her office, withdrawing a full ring of keys that jangle in her grasp. She pulls open the heavy door, and her head jerks when she looks outside. She recovers her stiff bearing and steps forward to confer with the visitors. I strain my ears, but only

4

murmurs reach me. Then Signora steps back and admits the callers. I press my face between the slats to see who they are.

As an older couple enters, Signora Silvia, the assistant to the prioress, joins Signora Priora below. The visitors have with them a young girl covered in a tattered shawl, its color calling to mind a bruised and overripe plum. I guess from her size that the girl is three or four years younger than I am—probably ten or eleven— but she keeps her head bowed, and I can't see her face. Signora Silvia reaches to push back the girl's head covering, and her hand recoils. Because the girl keeps her head down, I still cannot see what she looks like, what has prompted Signora Silvia, kind as she is, to shrink back from the girl.

Signora composes herself and smoothes the shawl around the child's shoulders. Signora Priora remains impassive during this exchange. Signora Silvia speaks to the old couple, and snatches of conversation drift up the stairwell. I hear words and phrases: "fire," "parents dead," and "cannot feed her." Then silence fills the space while Signora Priora folds her arms and contemplates what she has been told.

Catherine looks at me with her brows furrowed in puzzlement. I silently agree with her that this is an unusual situation. Ours is not the only *ospedale* in Venice. There are three others as well. Typically, our *Pietá* takes in only babies—babies who grow, when fate is kind, into children, and then young adults. Each week several infants are abandoned, as I was years ago, in the *scaffetta*, or revolving basket on the side street. Someone rings the bell and runs, and one of the matrons brings in the deserted baby. This girl, though, is not an infant and should be taken to one of the other *ospedali*.

Signora Priora happens to look up, still serious in thought, and squints as she catches my eye. She has caught us

5

eavesdropping. She holds my gaze for a long calculating moment, and I do not look away. Then she turns her gaze to the young girl and nods. "Yes," she says. "Yes, it is the right thing."

Signora Silvia snaps her head toward her superior and raises her eyebrows in surprise. "But the governors..." she stammers.

"Yes, Signora Silvia," affirms the prioress, "God has delivered this child to us, and I believe there is a reason for it."

"Of course," agrees the assistant. "I did not mean to question your judgment. It is just a little unusual..." And her words trail off.

"What can you tell me about her?" Signora Priora asks in her no-nonsense tone, directing her question to the two who hover near the girl.

The older couple appear poor, probably from a farming area on the mainland, and their voices are neither distinct nor loud. But the woman's voice rings clear when she states, "The girl's name is Monica." Then she adds, "Please do not change her name. It is the name given to her by her mother. It is who she is."

"So, Monica," says Signora Priora, "you shall remain with us now at the *Pietà*. Is she baptized?" she asks the couple.

"Yes, yes," they murmur. Signora nods her approval.

"Then her name shall remain Monica."

Signora reaches, I think gently, for Monica's chin and lifts the girl's face. When I see it, I raise my hand to my mouth to stifle a scream. Catherine draws a deep, sharp breath. I am paralyzed in horror as I look down at the child with the face so cruelly attacked by flame. Puckers of scars mar her skin from forehead to chin. She has no eyebrows or eyelashes, but worst of all, her lips have been almost obliterated. My first thought,

6

empty and silly as it is, is that this girl can never play a wind instrument like Catherine's oboe.

Signora Priora is still touching Monica when the prioress looks up again and sees that we remain on the landing above. Signora faintly nods her head before looking back to the girl. The peasant woman reaches for the burned waif and hugs her long and hard, stroking her back.

No one has ever hugged me like that.

"It is for the best," the old woman says, her voice trembling. Her companion gently pulls her away, and he pats Monica's shoulder. I catch my breath and wonder how they can leave her, for I can see they love her.

They turn toward the door, but Monica—they said her own mother gave her that name—never responds in any way to their departure. Signora Silvia ushers the couple out, but Monica just stands there, still and silent.

Signora Priora pulls her key and moves to lock the door upon her assistant's return and says, "Signora Silvia, I know it is normally your task to do so, but I will personally record this one's arrival."

I nudge Catherine, and we retreat into the rehearsal hall. Catherine's eyes are wet and shiny.

"How could she still be alive?" whispers Catherine. "How could she have survived when she was burned so badly?" She shivers. "I have never seen anyone like her."

I shrug my shoulders and voice the observation that bothers me the most right now. "She didn't cry. Did you notice? Her people left her here, and she didn't even cry. They abandoned her, and she did not act mad or sad, or anything." I bite my lip as a tear slides down my cheek. I hardly ever cry.

7

"Maybe she can't," says Catherine. "Maybe after the fire, she cried and cried for her mother, but when her mother never came back, she stopped crying altogether."

I nod with understanding at this explanation. Cecilia, my cello teacher, has told me that it is very important to respond and take care of babies and little ones when they cry, because when a child cries in vain, it will eventually give up and cry no more. Cecilia is four years older than I, and she knows more than any other girl here. I think this must be the saddest state of being—not bothering to cry because there is no hope of a response. I feel sorry for poor Monica—burned and abandoned and unable to cry. And then a most disturbing thought makes me reach to caress my left shoulder.

Catherine's eyes widen in horror as she realizes what I'm thinking. "Do you think they will brand her?" she asks with a note of anguish. "Hasn't that girl suffered enough?"

I shake my head and unthinkingly rub my left shoulder. "Let me see," implores Catherine, and I do not stop her when she pushes my sleeve all the way up my arm. There on the fleshy spot of my upper arm is my brand, my "P" seared into my flesh, forever marking me as a ward of the *Pietà*. For whatever reason, Catherine does not have the mark, and she has always had a morbid fascination with mine and the other girls'. I have no memory of receiving it, as odd as that sounds, for it must have been very painful at the time to have the white-hot iron put to my flesh. I've never heard of one other girl who remembers the branding either.

Moments later, as we sneak into the back of the chapel, late indeed for vespers, I ponder the mystery of the new girl. Instead of paying attention to the prayers, I ask myself why Signora Priora would take in that burned girl when she is supposed to take in just babies. I bite my lip as I wonder if Signora's curious action could have anything to do with me.

# Chapter Two
## *Seeking Trouble*

"Why would Signora Priora take her in?" I ask.

The puzzle of the new girl named Monica still crowds my thoughts when Catherine and I are served our supper.

Catherine shrugs. "Not for us to worry about, Isabella. Don't go seeking trouble. We were lucky enough that we didn't get in trouble earlier." She raises a spoonful of stew to her mouth but speaks before eating, "You should stop picking at your food and eat, or you'll be sorry tomorrow when your stomach is grumbling."

She is right. I should eat all that I have because Ash Wednesday, the beginning of Lent, is tomorrow. After tonight we won't have meat again until Easter, but my curiosity about the new arrival overshadows my appetite. I steal glances at all the tables, but I don't see the new girl. My bowl is still half full, shreds of beef floating in the stew, when Cecilia approaches me.

"Isabella," she says softly, "I have a message for you. Signora Priora wants you to come to her office as soon as you finish supper."

I gulp and shake off the apprehension that engulfs me. "Catherine and I must be in trouble for being late to vespers," I answer. "We'll go see her as soon as we finish."

"No," corrects Cecilia. "Just you. She did not say anything about Catherine."

I look up at Cecilia questioningly. With sympathy in her eyes, she shrugs gracefully. "I do not know, but just be strong, *Piccola Gatta*."

The softness in Cecilia's voice, along with the use of her pet name for me, Little Cat, unnerves me. Any remaining appetite is gone, and I know I may as well go ahead and face my consequence, but my consequence for what? Is tardiness a sin, and if so, would that be a venial sin or a mortal sin? And why am I the only one in trouble? I try to scoot off the bench without jostling my companions, but Catherine reaches over and squeezes my hand.

"I don't understand why it should be only you," she says, comforting me, "but you'll be okay. You always are. Let me know what happens."

I know, of course, that this summons is about a sin greater than being late to vespers.

With heavy feet I leave the dining hall, passing the chess table on my way. I trudge toward the foyer where Monica was admitted earlier. Signora's office sits to the side of the building, directly off the entry hall. I pause before her door, consider again the events that transpired here a short while ago, and I rap gently.

"Come in, Isabella dal Cello. Do not dawdle." Her voice is crisp and firm. She looks up from her journal and lays down her quill. Her pristine white cap frames her face. She squeezes her eyes shut, then opens them widely as though she is trying to bring me into focus.

I drop my eyes to the floor and shuffle forward, but then a feisty impulse straightens my backbone. I look the woman straight in her eyes. She does not have a real name—she is known by the job she does. She is the prioress who is in charge of us all.

"You asked for me, Signora Priora," I state, not waiting for her invitation to speak. This kind of boldness is quite inappropriate.

*Clack...clack...clack.* Her teeth rap an annoyed rhythm, but she keeps her gaze locked on mine.

"You anger me, Isabella dal Cello," Signora Priora says flatly. She taps the journal with her finger, a ledger filled with numbers. "But," she continues, "I will not let my emotion get in the way of what is best for the *Pietà*. Yesterday I fed 712 hungry souls and today I fed 713. Tomorrow—who knows? If this were about only you, I would send you away."

My heart slams in my chest as I recall how Signora promised additional retribution after my sin during *Carnevale*. I hoped she would forget, but, of course, she has not. Clearly, the rage she felt that night when she caught Catherine and me sneaking back into the courtyard is with her still.

"You are valuable," the prioress continues, "because you are a good musician. The orchestra brings in donations that help feed everyone, and I am not blind to the fact that Don Vivaldi considers you an important part of the orchestra." She taps the journal before her. "But understand clearly that nothing is about you. Everything I do is for the whole."

She is not going to send me away, but what then? I hold my tongue.

"You are arrogant," she says, staring me down, "and you are selfish. These traits made you foolish a couple of weeks ago. I will not allow you to risk the reputation of the *Pietà* again, but I have been vexed trying to figure out how to reform your attitude—that is, I have been vexed until today."

She wags her finger at me. "Today God answered my prayers, and I know what needs to be done with you."

13

I stand mute. What response can I offer? I believe I am neither arrogant nor selfish.

"Today we took in a new girl, a girl named Monica." And then quite unexpectedly, Signora adds a sincere question. "What did you think of the new girl when you saw her?"

I purse my lips as I frame an answer. "You might think me foolish and simple-minded, but when I saw that her lips had been burned so badly, I knew she could never play a wind instrument."

"I do not think you foolish, because I myself made the same observation." Signora looks from me to her long outstretched fingers and studies them. "I examined her, Isabella, and her hands are fine. Her fingers were not damaged in the fire. It is a miracle, is it not?"

Signora looks back at me, but I know she does not really seek an answer. She continues, "So if she cannot play an oboe or flute, what might she be able to play?"

This time I respond, "Well, she could learn to play a violin or viola."

"Or she could learn to play the cello, could she not?"

I shrug. "She could, I guess."

At that, Signora Priora smiles broadly and triumphantly folds her arms, smirking as though she has put a chess opponent in checkmate. "She could indeed learn to play the cello, Isabella, and you will be the one to teach her."

"M....m...me?" I stammer. "But I do not know how to be a teacher. Surely this is not my job."

"Then you will learn to be a teacher," she retorts smugly, "and it will indeed be your job." Signora Priora lays out a plan, and I listen in a fog of disbelief. She charges me with a responsibility that will steal precious hours from my days, and then she dismisses me with an imperious wave of her hand. Stunned, I walk out her door and she says to my back, "We are all teachers in one way or another."

I stumble in anger through the foyer because Signora Priora is trying to ruin me! I have my dream, and she seeks to destroy it. I want to be so good that Don Vivaldi will write a cello concerto that features me. She knows that I need to spend every spare moment practicing with my Speranza—not taking care of that new girl. I do feel sorry for Monica, but she cannot be my responsibility.

With heat burning in my cheeks, I step into a secluded alcove beneath the staircase to gather my wits. My breathing calms, and I rest here, appreciating the solid wall supporting my back. Tender strains of violin music drift down the stairwell. Someone, probably the *maestro* himself, is practicing in our rehearsal hall on the fourth floor. Don Antonio Vivaldi frequently takes up his violin in the evening before he goes home. I close my eyes and let my head sway with the melody. The haunting flow of minor notes circles me, consumes me, and takes me back to that evening.

They are so clear, my memories of what happened eleven days ago. I remember with vivid detail the events, the feelings, the choices I made that day—no, I do not regret anything I did. I am not sorry for sneaking out that night and taking Catherine with me. That is why in good conscience I have not been able to go to the confessional and ask forgiveness. I am not sorry.

Now I must face the consequences of breaking the rules. I have to go upstairs and take on the duty of caring for Monica's life, all of it. Signora Priora would never, ever have accepted Monica in the *Pietà* if our prioress had not desired to punish me in the cruelest manner.

## ISABELLA'S LIBRETTO

Propelled by the emotion of the violin solo, I sigh deeply and move from the alcove. I place my hand on the rail and take a daunting look at the thirty stairs ascending to the dormitory — and Monica. And I take the first step.

# Chapter Three
## *The Punishment*

*Wicked*, she said. As I climb the stairs, I cannot help but remember that Signora Priora called me wicked that night when she caught Catherine and me. But truly, I am no such thing. I longed to see the fireworks, have an adventure beyond our cloistered walls, and yes, I convinced Catherine to come with me. It would have been selfish to go without her!

After the fireworks, of course, things did not go as we planned, but we did make it back to the *ospedale* unharmed. Signora Priora was waiting for us, though, as soon as we slipped back into the courtyard. That memory comes to life as I climb, and I pause on the stairway landing, reliving the confrontation in my mind.

*"Where have you been?"*

*The deep velvet darkness of the night renders Signora Priora invisible, but her restrained anger creates a palpable presence in the seclusion of our courtyard. The night sounds are low, leaving the administrator's accusing question hanging heavy in the air. With my heart still racing from our earlier terror, I almost let a wave of defeat wash over me now that we are discovered by the woman who controls our lives. But I will not cry. I will not cry. No, I will not cry.*

*I can barely see Catherine next to me, but I know her shoulders slump. "We...left," she says haltingly.*

*"Indeed," replies Signora. "You left. You broke all the rules. You defied not only my authority, but that of the board of governors as well. But worst of all, you compromised the welfare of all the other girls."*

"But…how?" I stammer. Her accusation startles me. "We would never do anything to hurt our friends!"

Clack…clack…clack. Signora strikes her teeth together, a habit she displays when especially offended. "You are so foolish," she says. "Did you go to the Piazza to see the fireworks? Is that the temptation that lured you away?"

I feel rather than see her stepping closer to us. "Yes," I croak, "we went to the Piazza."

"You went to the Piazza," she repeats, "and it never once occurred to you that you might be risking the reputation of the Pietá?"

Catherine and I both remain silent because we truly do not know what she is talking about.

"Did you know," she demands, "that your daily bread is provided by benefactors who would not feel so charitable if the Pietá were tainted by the scandal of young wards running around without proper chaperones?"

"Did you know," she continues, "that there are several marriage contracts under negotiation for some of the older girls? These marriages would be good for the girls and good for the Pietá. Do you know why respectable families come to our ospedale to find wives? Because our ospedale has a strong reputation for protecting the virtue of its girls, and this, THIS in your thoughtless selfishness, you have risked tonight."

"But we are fine," Catherine hastens to explain. "There was no harm. We got away from them!"

Signora draws a sharp breath as her hand flies to her chest, inadvertently knocking the rosary beads at her waist. "What do you mean, Caterina? Got away from whom?"

Next to me, Catherine bristles at the sound of the Italian variation of her name. I hasten to provide an explanation.

"Truly, we were not violated. And nobody knew who we were."

18

*Signora puts her face close to mine and restrains my shoulders. "Your personal welfare is not my worry right now," she says with eyes boring into mine. "My worry is the welfare of hundreds of children — hundreds of girls and boys who might not have enough to eat if our patrons get whiff of a scandal and do not contribute generously to us. Without omitting one detail, tell me exactly what happened after you left the Pietá."*

*And we do. Catherine and I recount the threatening events of the evening. At the end of our tale, Signora Priora shakes her head, her lips pursed in frustration. Finally, she speaks.*

*"You are clever. You are both so clever, and so pretty, and such fine musicians. And yet you are selfish and egocentric." She raises her hands, palms open in front of us. "God give me the wisdom of Solomon to figure out how to deal with the likes of you."*

*Then she appraises us in the faint light, slowly looking us up and down, trying to come up with just the right form of punishment. My heart thuds in my chest anticipating the unknown. Catherine's breathing accelerates, and once again tonight, I feel the need to protect her.*

*"It was my fault, Signora Priora," I confess. "It was all my idea, not Catherine's. Please do not hurt her."*

*Signora nods. "I believe you, Isabella. I expected that you were the wicked one who instigated this rebellious behavior. Nonetheless, you went along with it, Caterina. You share the guilt."*

*I steal a look at Catherine to gauge her reaction, and I can tell she clenches her jaw when she is called Caterina. I then look at Signora, and I detect a smirk. She knows how much Catherine hates to be called that other name.*

*"So," Signora says, "the two of you will spend the remainder of the night kneeling in contrition before the altar. You will not sit. You will not lie down. No — you will kneel and ask God to show you the*

*selfishness of your ways so that you can truly repent and ask forgiveness for your sin. You will be denied breakfast in the morning, but you will attend prayers and practice your music as usual."*

*I wait because I expect there must be something more—something horrible, perhaps a switching or whipping. The three of us stand speechless for what seems like several minutes. Impatient as I am, I finally ask, "Is that all, Signora?"*

*"Not likely," she retorts. "God's mercy is great, but mine is not. Your night in the church will not satisfy your debt to me. I will think on the matter and let you know what further consequence you will suffer. And you will."*

Now, Signora Priora has found the punishment she sought. The girl named Monica will be my consequence to suffer. My fingernails dig into the heels of my palms. Signora Priora knows—of course she knows—that I have no time to take on additional responsibility. I practice more than any other girl in the orchestra because I have a goal, and Signora Priora, with her wretched attempt to reform me, will not keep me from working toward my dream. She says I will teach the new girl how to play the cello, and not only that, but Signora wants me to tutor the girl in basic academic studies.

Well, I will not fail. I knelt all night in the church, didn't I, despite the miserable pain in my back and knees? I will show Signora Priora that I can fulfill the terms of her punishment and still be the best cellist in the Pietá.

"Isabella."

The soft whisper of my name intrudes on my thoughts, and I look up to see Catherine leaning over the banister and motioning.

"Come," she says. "You will not believe what you see."

20

# Chapter Four
## *Teachers*

I hurry up the stairs and join my friend on the landing of the second floor.

"Are you okay?" she queries with concern.

"I'm fine," I bite out. "She is not going to keep me from doing what I long to do."

"Oh, but wait until you see what she has done, at least I think it must be Signora Priora's doing."

Following Catherine's lead, I tiptoe into the dormitory where several other girls have already gone to sleep. Startled, I see that another body has been placed in the bed I share with Gabriella, also a cellist. A shapeless lump rests at the edge under the wool blanket. Gabriella snores lightly on the other side.

"Look," Catherine whispers, and she draws me closer to the new inhabitant. "She has put Monica in your bed."

"Yes, it is no surprise," I say, shaking my head. "Signora Priora says I have to take care of her and be her teacher."

With a morbid curiosity I step close to look down at her. Two lamps still burn in the room, so I can distinguish in the dim light the horrible disfigurement of her face. Minute after minute I study her, noticing how her small chest barely rises and falls under the covers with each thin breath she takes. She is now my responsibility. If she ever cries, I am the one who will have to take care of her.

I ease back the edge of the blanket so I can push up the left sleeve of her night shift. Quietly, oh so quietly, Catherine leans

21

forward with me, and we see that the tender flesh of her shoulder has not been seared with a fresh brand.

"Thank you, Holy Mother," I breathe.

I cannot stop my hand as it reaches down to her arm. I stroke Monica's surprisingly smooth flesh above her elbow, and I cannot reconcile it with the roughness of her face and head. Her eyes remain closed, and her breathing maintains its shallow rhythm.

I tug the sleeve of her shift down to her wrist and take one of her fingers in my grasp. Her finger is long and slender, and I rub my thumb over the half moon of a ragged fingernail. I lean close to see that the underside of her nail is dirt-stained, so she must have worked the earth. Still, she gives no evidence of awakening.

I look up at Catherine, whose attention is focused on Monica's head. "We need to check," whispers Catherine, and I agree.

"I'll do it," I say. I pause before placing both my hands on Monica's scalp. Sparse tufts of hair sprout from her puckered flesh like dandelion puffs resting on tree bark. Bending close to see in the weak light, I inspect the roots and fine shafts of her hair. Catherine smiles at me when I nod and say, "She is clean."

We battle lice here, so it is essential that someone check Monica to make sure she does not harbor the pests. Even though she worked with her hands before, someone must have cared for Monica and seen to her hygiene. Now that task falls to me.

Looking back down, Catherine gently lays her hand on Monica's shoulder. "Isabella, you won't be mean to her, will you?"

I shake my head. "Catherine, please don't think that. I'm not mean—I just don't have time."

When I climb into bed later, Monica's ragged breaths brush my ear, and I fall into a fitful sleep wedged between her and Gabriella.

The next morning, a cold blanket of fog enshrouds Venice, keeping us all in near darkness even though it is time to get up. As always, the bells ring and call us to our daily tasks. I have dreamed, again, of playing Speranza in one of Vivaldi's concertos, so a smile hovers on my lips as I rise through the depths of consciousness. But before I break the surface, reality jolts me awake, and I turn to look.

Yes, there is a third body in our bed, and Monica is next to me. After I rub the sleep from my eyes, I reach and grab her shoulder.

"You have to wake up now," I command. She does not respond. "Monica," I say her name, "please, wake up. We have to get ready."

For a moment, I am afraid she has died during the night because her breathing is barely audible. But then she turns her head and opens her eyes, looking up at the ceiling with a vacant stare. I hate to push back the covers because it is so cold, but I nudge Gabriella and follow her out of her side of the bed. I walk around and pull back the blanket from Monica. A simple dark red woolen dress, the uniform here in the *Pietá*, lies across the end of the bed, along with a white apron and white shawl collar. One of the matrons must have brought the clothing after I went to sleep. I look right down in Monica's face, and I do not flinch.

"Signora Priora says I have to take care of you," I tell her. "You don't need to be afraid. Nobody here will hurt you."

She says not one word to me as we slip on our plain dresses, wash our faces in the icy cold water in the basin, and go

23

downstairs. Several of the other girls stop with sudden shock when they see Monica's horrid face, but nobody laughs or snickers at her. Most of us have marks left by the pox, but nothing as awful as her scars.

"Are you not able to speak?" I ask. She remains mute and her face remains blank of all expression, but she obeys, without fail, all my requests.

Because it is Ash Wednesday, our first obligation is to join the others in the church to receive the black smudges on our foreheads, the mark that signifies that we have all come from dust, and to dust we shall one day return. I nudge Monica in front of me in the line of girls approaching the altar, and when the priest anoints her furrowed forehead with the ashes, I notice that she doesn't flinch. The priest doesn't either. When the service is over, I take her hand and lead her back to the *ospedale* and up to the rehearsal hall. I have to slow my pace so that she can keep up with me as we climb the three flights of stairs.

"Everyone here has a job," I explain. "Every person here has to earn her keep in some way or another. Some work in the laundry, some in the kitchen. Some learn to make lace and some learn to be seamstresses. Some of the girls have the honored job of embroidering altar cloths and vestments for priests. Oh, and there are boys as well, but they live in another building. We never see them, not even at church. They are kept completely away from us, and of course, they have jobs as well—but the boys have no orchestra."

I pause to catch my breath and notice that she is breathing much more heavily than I. Unable to restrain my proud smile, I continue, "But I am in the orchestra, *una figlia del coro*, a daughter of the choir. My cello sings, and my job here is to be the best cellist I can be. And you are very lucky, Monica, because you

24

have been assigned to the orchestra too, if you can learn to play the cello."

"Sit in this chair," I instruct her. "I'm the one who will teach you to play the cello, the instrument that I play. I've named my cello Speranza."

Her eyes regard me vacantly as I continue, "Maybe the best way to begin lessons is for you to observe me and listen to me play for a few days. That way you can learn what a cello is supposed to sound like."

I sit close to her, withdraw Speranza from her leather case, and nestle the instrument between my calves. I take my bow and tighten the horsehair strings. "Watch how I do this," I command. I glance at her slyly to make sure she is watching me. As I practice scales for the next half hour, she sits rigid, never moving her head, even to see who is entering the room. Other girls come and go, several stay and play, and the hall is filled with the various notes and melodies of intense practice. Monica never takes her eyes off me, yet I feel as though she doesn't see me.

After some time, Cecilia enters and approaches. "I see you have a cello student, Isabella." Cecilia kneels in front of Monica's stool and looks her right in the eyes. "Monica, you have a good teacher."

Monica simply stares back at Cecilia. Unperturbed, Cecilia adds with a grin, "You have a good teacher, because she has a good teacher." Cecilia then lays her hands on both sides of Monica's face and traces her fingers lightly over the ridged skin of her cheeks. She runs her hands down the sleeves of Monica's dress and takes Monica's hands in her own, rubbing her thumbs up and down each of Monica's unblemished fingers.

"You have good fingers," says Cecilia, "good, strong fingers to play the cello."

I think Monica's misshapen mouth turns slightly up into a hint of a smile. Cecilia turns from Monica, winks at me, and pulls a third bench closer. "Now, Isabella, you and I need to get busy on your lesson."

"Yes," I agree, "but first, please excuse me for just a moment."

I go to the instrument cabinet and find the smaller scale cello on which I first learned to play. I place it on the floor beside Monica and guide her hands to the neck of the instrument. "Just hold it while Cecilia and I have our lesson," I instruct her. "Feel the wood in your hands, and let your fingers feel the gut of the strings. And you can give this cello a name if you want to."

Cecilia nods approvingly. "You will be a good teacher, Isabella. The *Pietà* will need more teachers. I will be proud to pass you along."

"What do you mean?" I ask sharply. "Don't you want to be my teacher anymore? I've done so well lately."

Cecilia shakes her head as though responding to a simpleton. "Silly Isabella," she says, "of course you've done well. You are playing so well that Don Vivaldi has taken note. You are doing so well that you're about to pass me by, and then I can't be your teacher anymore. Don Vivaldi himself will soon be your teacher."

Stunned, I feel as though the breath has been sucked out of me at the thought that Cecilia might not be my teacher anymore. I should be happy, giddy even, at Cecilia's praise and the possibility that the *maestro* himself might be instructing me, but for reasons I can't articulate, I feel lost. I look at Monica and notice that instead of looking at me, she is concentrating on her fingers caressing the strings of the cello.

I can hardly remember when that small cello was first placed in my hands, but I do remember the contentment I felt the day I first had a lesson with Cecilia. I had a happy sense of belonging, a sense of friendship with Cecilia that has grown over the years we have worked together. I am not sure how she came to know, but it was Cecilia who told me that I had been left at the *Pietà* sometime in 1702. It surprises me still how much I treasure even that tiny scrap of information about my arrival at the *Pietà*.

My indefinable sadness at the prospect of losing Cecilia as my teacher chips away at my concentration. Instead of focusing on my cello, I let my eyes travel around the large music hall and notice Catherine practicing with some woodwinds. Then, I gaze at the tall windows that look beyond our city of islands and canals to the lagoon in the distance, and I am distracted by the movement of sails there. Never have I been allowed to venture to the mainland, and often those sails lure my imagination to the possibilities beyond Venice. I know that I should be focusing on my lesson, at least thinking about Monica, but a gray and depressing gloom dampens my enthusiasm for my music. Sometimes even a disciplined musician loses her concentration.

Frustrated with my poor attempts, I lay down Speranza and my bow. "Please, Cecilia," I say, "I need a moment."

I wander over to a window, its wavy panes of glass splotched with water droplets. Dark leaden clouds hang heavy in the sky, and an oppressive mist hangs over the city. The cold moisture sneaks in the doors, penetrates the walls, and cloaks us all with an inescapable wet chill.

I sigh and look to the pennants hanging limp on the ships in the distance. On a breezy sun-struck day, the banners dance with vivid color against the sparkling water, but on a dull day such as this, they hover with a colorless ghostlike quality against the graphite sheets of water that stretch across the horizon. Looking closer, just below, I see that even the *fondamenta* is now deserted, the throng of city visitors chased inside by the gloom of the dark morning.

Cecilia silently steps up to join me, and her breath exhales with a hint of sadness as she gazes out to the great lagoon that leads to the sea. Monica follows her, and she stands on the other side of me. Cecilia raises her dimpled chin thoughtfully, allowing the neat braid of her cinnamon-hued hair to cascade farther down the back of her plain woolen smock. "Bleak days such as this always make me think of the dead babies," she murmurs.

The curious statement falls heavily on the silence, and my shoulders hunch with an involuntary shiver. "Dead babies," I parrot. "What dead babies?"

She keeps her eyes trained on the horizon. "We are here because of the dead babies."

I look at Cecilia with wide eyes, and then put an arm protectively around Monica's shoulders. "What dead babies, Cecilia?" I ask, my voice rising in agitation. She is only a few years older than I, but I am accustomed to giving her the respect due one's mentor. In this matter, however, I don't understand her, and I don't like the gravity in her voice.

"It really is true," she replies, turning toward me. "The fishermen used to haul up dead babies in their nets."

Pinpricks of goose flesh rise on my arms and neck as she points to the menacing water. "Imagine the horror," she says, "of discovering a tiny blue corpse in your net. It happened all the time."

"How do you know such an awful thing?" I demand.

Cecilia shrugs. "One of the older girls told me, much as I am telling you…and Monica. I imagine that one day you will pass the story along to some of the younger ones." She smiles mysteriously. "That is the way of things here, you know. We pass our knowledge along, one girl to another."

So engrossed am I in Cecilia's horrid story that I hardly notice when Catherine steps up to join our little group looking out the window. Wide-eyed, I look at my best friend to acknowledge her presence. Then I look at Monica beside me, and she returns my interest. For the first time I feel that my eyes really connect with Monica's.

"So what happened?" I ask.

"Our wise rulers of Venice decided something had to be done. You see, the problem was this: unmarried girls, sometimes the daughters of important families, would conceive children, and as you can surely understand, this would mean the ruin of the girls and a stain on the family name."

I understand, and I nod knowingly. Monica, of course, cannot possibly understand yet. Signora Priora would never, ever discuss where babies come from, but as Cecilia has alluded to, in this place the girls share their knowledge as big sister to little sister. I have learned, with some astonishment, how babies come to be.

"So what happened?" I ask again.

"So the women, or maybe someone else, would sometimes throw their babies out a window into the water below. It probably wasn't just girls from titled families, but other women as well, poor women, who found themselves unable to feed their babies. It happened so frequently that the city decided to establish a great hospital with a hundred wet nurses, women who were feeding their own babies and agreed to nurse an abandoned infant as well." She nods her head. "That is the story of our *Pietà*."

Like a magnet, the frigid steel-colored water draws my gaze, and I shudder. "It could've been you and me," I mutter.

I feel an arm go around my waist, and Monica draws closer to me.

"Oh, it probably would've been you and me," Cecilia agrees. "After all, where did we come from? Where did the others come from? But we were saved because Venice built our *ospedale* and the three others."

With her typical grace and detachment, Cecilia walks away and leaves me at the window with Monica and Catherine. I strengthen my hold on Monica with my right arm and put my left arm around Catherine's shoulders. It's too much to think about right now. I look down upon Monica sheltered at my side, and the weight of my responsibility presses on my shoulders, forcing from the depths of my being a sigh of resignation.

"Isabella," Catherine whispers in my ear. "The fireworks— were they worth the price?"

And I ask myself the same question.

# Chapter Five

## *Fireworks*

The price I will pay is named Monica. What experience did I purchase that night that lives so vivid in my memory? The events began right here in this very rehearsal hall. Twelve days ago I made a choice that has resulted in a serious consequence. I look around, and in my mind's eye I see the details with great clarity, and I feel the energy of that afternoon pulsing in this space.

*On that afternoon, Don Antonio Vivaldi keeps our orchestra longer at practice than we are scheduled. I know he is pleased with our efforts. When he looks at the sixty of us, he sees musicians, not just orphan girls. We play the last measure of his composition, again, and we wait. He has taken us through the last movement at least five times, and I feel we are perfect on this last attempt.*

*I hold my breath expectantly and keep my eyes on him. He is not wearing his white wig today, so his russet locks fall to his shoulders, and one stray strand of perspiration-soaked hair brushes his broad hook nose. His breathing is heavy—he is a very energetic maestro who conducts with bold sweeps of his arms—but now his shoulders are rigid, and he keeps his arms poised in the air. The dimple in his chin twitches ever so slightly. His eyes deliberately move over all the instruments, assessing, evaluating. We hold a collective breath.*

*Then his solemn demeanor explodes into one of triumph. "Bravissime, my girls! Today, you play like angels!" He raises his hands to us, palms up, in a gesture of affirmation. "All of Venice will celebrate you on Sunday. You are angel musicians," he adds, looking around the circle of the seated orchestra with pride. I exhale and let a tremor of exhilaration snake down my spine.*

*I am a figlia del coro, not a daughter of a mother, but a daughter of a choir—a musician who sings with her instrument rather than her voice. I value order, discipline, and conformity, but this afternoon I indulgently let a wave of joy wash over me, because soon I will be the chosen one! This Sunday it will be Annamaria who will play the solo on her violin during the concerto, but I am getting better every day. Don Antonio will soon notice that I am just as good on my cello as Annamaria is on her violin, and he will reward me with a concerto. This is my dream.*

*I lovingly hold the neck of Speranza and gently run my fingers over the strings while Don Vivaldi's praise echoes in my head: "Bravissime!" A sense of jubilation wells up within, and I feel a pulse of satisfaction coursing through the whole room.*

*On this note, I hear the whisper of a forbidden inner voice. This temptation has tickled the edge of my conscience before, but this time I yield and entertain it. I look around the hall, and the other girls, all looking happy, are rustling music, putting away instruments, and chatting gaily. Do they hear it too? This forbidden voice entices me: "Fireworks!"*

*I tell the temptation to go away, but it does not. I confess that I have thought about it before.*

*Here in Venice, the short, dark days of winter are enlivened by the parties of Carnevale. The revelry must stop, of course, on Ash Wednesday, when Lent begins. But until then, while the cold rains shroud our island in gloom, the winter-weary inhabitants and visitors fight the misery of the weather with costumed celebrations and merriment of all sorts. I think the best entertainment of all must surely be the fireworks! Even though I am rarely allowed to venture beyond the sheltered walls of our ospedale, I know that almost every night during the season there is a dazzling display of fireworks in the Piazza San Marco. I have never seen them, but we hear visitors talk about them. People gesture excitedly with their hands and arms, and their voices rise to a crescendo when they describe the great spectacle of fireworks. It is innocent, isn't it, to want to see such a wonder for myself? To embark on this grand adventure—dare I?*

*I look at Catherine, sitting with the other wind players. Her instrument is still out. Right now she is the only oboist in our orchestra. The older oboist, Lorenza, recently left to get married, and the two younger ones will need many months of practice before they are good enough to join us in public performances. Catherine is a very, very good musician, but she's an even better friend.*

*I take a breath and lift my bow with my right hand. I slide the bow across the strings, almost in a feathery whisper, while my left hand forms the chords. The five-note phrase in a minor key drifts across the room. With all the commotion, no one notices—no one, that is, except Catherine. She answers my gaze with a questioning look, and then she smiles furtively. Catherine picks up her oboe and echoes the same haunting notes in the same minor key. As I wipe the horsehair strings of my bow with my faded red silk cloth, I smile to myself, because I know the effect the secret signal will bring. The adventure is begun. I bite my lip.*

*On this morning, I had risen before dawn and gone upstairs to practice before morning prayers, not because I had to, but because I yearned to be perfect in today's rehearsal. I had gone to class and conjugated most of my Latin verbs without error. And then I missed not one answer when Signora Marta quizzed me on my multiplication tables. I am a good and obedient student, but now there is a giddy sense of freedom beckoning me. So I take a breath, a very deep breath, and go down the stairs one flight to my dormitory. I share it with a dozen other girls, but I'm the only one here now. Lucky for me, the others must have gone straight to the dining hall. The lid on my worn wooden chest creaks with complaint when I open it to retrieve my brown woolen cloak, and the sound startles me. I glance over my shoulder, but I'm still alone. I grab my cloak, my mantella, and tiptoe over to Catherine's chest and get hers. My heart starts to race now as I slip down the back stairs, holding my bundle of mud-colored wool close to my chest. I pause in alarm when I encounter Gabriella and Valeria on the landing, but I find my composure. I raise my head and say, "Buonasera."*

*At the bottom of the stairs, I ease out of the doorway and into the courtyard. Now I breathe. My eyes adjust to the dim grayness that is quickly enveloping the walled space, and then I make my way to the pomegranate tree, where I wait and review my plan. I also recall the map of Venice that I have studied in the classroom, and I concentrate on remembering the location of every canal and alleyway between here and the Piazza San Marco. A dove calls, and in my best imitation of a dove, I answer. Catherine emerges from the shadows and scurries to my side.*

*"You came!" I say, smiling in relief.*

*"What are we doing? What's this about?" The anticipation in her voice indicates she's keen on what I have to say.*

*"Fireworks," I answer, with a suggestive raise of an eyebrow.*

*She brings a hand to her mouth in a gesture of delight. "The ones in the Piazza San Marco?"*

*I nod eagerly. "How many times have we been stuck in our rooms when we could hear the explosions? Boom! Boom! Boom! Boom!" I punctuate each word by punching the air with alternate fists, and Catherine fights to restrain a full laugh.*

*"Shh," she cautions with a big smile.*

*"Can you remember," I ask, "how we craned our necks out the window to see the fireworks, but we couldn't see anything at all?" I*

lower my voice to a bare whisper. "We can go see the fireworks tonight!"

Catherine stands silent for some moments, and then shakes her head, "No we can't. We could get in trouble, big trouble."

"I want to go—I'll go without you."

She considers my claim, and then asks, "How can we manage such a thing?"

"I have a plan," I say, with more bravado than my thumping heart feels.

"Do you have a plan that can get by Signora Priora?"

The very mention of our prioress casts a pall over my eagerness, but I recover my shaky confidence. "For the plan to work, we'll have to completely avoid Signora Priora, but I think we can do that. We'll miss supper, of course, but what's food compared to going to the fireworks for the first time in our lives? I'll go hungry for that!"

"Hmmm," she says. "I heard that we were going to get an extra serving of sweet bread tonight because Don Vivaldi is so pleased with us."

"I don't care about sweets tonight," I say. "I really am going to go."

"Isabella dal Cello, I do believe you'll go see the fireworks tonight, no matter what. And can I let you go alone?" She purses her lips and wrinkles her nose. "The fireworks do sound so exciting! So what kind of plan have you come up with?"

Now that she has relented, I exhale the breath I've been holding, and I explain: "You'll pretend to be sick and ask to be excused from the dining hall so that you can go upstairs. And of course, you'll avoid Signora Priora. I'll find Signora Silvia and tell her I haven't done my penance from my confession last Saturday, and I want to go to the church for prayer and contemplation."

35

*Catherine stifles giggles and shakes her head. "That's truly the silliest thing I've ever heard. No one, not even Signora Silvia, would believe that of you." Then her eyes grow round with conspiratorial pleasure. "But she would believe it of me," she adds, "so I'll use that excuse. You'll have to pretend to be sick. Whoever is on duty in the dining hall this evening, just tell her that your stomach feels horrid and you have to go lie down."*

*After a few final whispered plans, we stash our balled-up cloaks beneath a stone bench and retreat to lay the groundwork for our evening out. As I enter the dining hall, I'm assailed by the tantalizing aroma of cinnamon and toasted almonds. In spite of the mouth-watering appeal, I find the matron monitoring the meal. Fortune smiles on me because it's someone I don't know well, so I don't feel very guilty telling her a mistruth. I hate it, though, when she responds with kindness to my dishonesty about being sick. "I am so sorry," she says, patting my shoulder. "Are you sure? Don Vivaldi has asked that the musicians get a very special treat tonight." Taking a deep whiff of the wonderful scent, I turn and leave the promised reward.*

*A few minutes later, Catherine meets me back in the courtyard, now almost completely dark. "It is done," she proclaims, "I am at this moment in the chapel praying." We find our cloaks under the bench and wrap them around us. I pause momentarily as I pull the hood up over my head, unable to ignore the cautionary voice within. "Catherine, are you sure?" I ask. "We could pay a high price."*

*She ponders my question, and then nods thoughtfully. "Yes, I am sure." She raises her chin and hums our five minor notes. I exhale in relief and respond in like manner.*

*We pull the folds of rough brown wool to cover our faces as best we can. My features are plainly nondescript: I have dirt brown hair and plain green eyes, lips that are too small and eyebrows that are too bushy. But Catherine has a pretty face with blue eyes. I reach over and tug the hood more closely over her white-blonde hair that frames her slender, ivory-fair face. I am thankful for our cloaks to disguise us, because it's very cold this February evening, and we'll be glad of our heavy woolen wraps to keep us warm as the air turns frigid.*

*All set, we silently slip out the gate to the small street. We start in the direction of the big canal, but realize simultaneously that we shouldn't go there. The Ospedale della Pietà sits right on the Canal di San Marco, and probably no fewer than twenty windows in the building look out over the wide landing there. "We need to take the back way to the Piazza," Catherine says in a low voice. "Someone might see us walking along the water. I hope you know where you're going in the dark."*

*Nodding my agreement, we reverse direction. It's one of many instances when we have the same thought at the same time. In doubling back, we pass the large bell mounted on the wall, the bell that mothers ring when they abandon their babies, and we exchange knowing glances. We hurry down the narrow passageway, edged with buildings three and four stories tall. It leads into the maze that is Venice, a maze that is crisscrossed by more than a hundred small canals. We turn left onto another dark alleyway, or calle, when the small street dead-ends, then shortly we go right again. Catherine makes another left, and comfortable now that we are beyond the range of apprehension, I laugh and grab at her arm.*

*"Where are you going?" I cry. "Do you want to end up bobbing in the water?" She has begun to go down a narrow walk that leads only to a gondola mooring on a waterway named the Rio dei Greci. In the dark it would be easy just to walk off into the stinky, murky little canal if you didn't know where you were going.*

*Answering my laugh, she replies, "It's very confusing here, but no, I certainly don't want to have to explain wet clothes tonight."*

*Now that we are away from the school, we are free to talk. "Look at us," I moan. "We're going to Carnevale, and we look like two drab mice that just crawled out of our hole."*

*"You, Isabella, are thinking like a schoolgirl," she chastises me, "but now we must think like the rich aristocrats we play music for every week."*

*"You don't think we look like mice?"*

*"Not at all," she says, grinning impishly. "I think we look like rich old ladies who are wearing costumes to make us look like innocent, even poor, orphaned schoolgirls."*

*I quickly capture her line of imagination. "I get it," I say. "We could be those snooty English ladies...."*

*"No!" she interrupts. "We're not going to make fun of the English." Her tone is serious, and I'm having too much fun to argue.*

*"Okay," I say. "Well, then, we can be duchesses from Vienna."*

*"Or better yet," Catherine suggests, "we'll be some of those ladies from Paris who wear the ridiculously big hairstyles that look like bird cages tottering on their heads. We decide that for one evening we want to go out without our big white wigs that are probably crawling with all sorts of creepy creatures."*

*"Oh, I like this game," I agree. "For tonight we'll pretend to be rich French women pretending to be poor orphans."*

*Catherine pats the side of her face. "Poor orphans from the Ospedale della Pietà who are young and innocent and beautiful."*

*We laugh together in rich camaraderie and adopt the proud and haughty posture of those we ridicule. To my chagrin, Catherine has grown faster than I have lately, and now she stands half a head taller as we attempt to stroll regally toward our destination.*

*Our spirits high with humor and excitement, we mix with the growing number of masqueraders making their way through the narrow streets until we come to the side of the Basilica di San Marco.*

*There we are jostled with the swarming crowd right into the Piazza itself. The incredible sight before us steals my breath.*

"Isabella, Isabella!" Catherine calls my name and calls me back to the present. I shake my head to clear it of the vivid image of the *Carnevale* celebration and feel a tug at my sleeve. I am startled when I look down at Monica and see she has opened her mouth to speak. My excitement that she'll no longer be silent pushes my memories of the fireworks into a back corner of my mind.

# Chapter Six
## *The Call of the Bells*

"I'm hungry," Monica says in a whisper. These are the first words she speaks to me.

A smile splits my face, but for a moment I cannot think what to say.

"Isabella." Studying my face, she says my name softly.

Monica's gray eyes grow round as she tests my name on her lips for a second time, this with more conviction: "Isabella."

"Yes," I say and nod my head. "I am Isabella."

She cocks her head with an unspoken question.

"I'm supposed to take care of you," I explain. Catherine clears her throat behind me, and I turn to her. "And this is my friend Catherine. She will be your friend too."

Monica frowns. "Cath—er—ine." She strings the syllables of the unfamiliar name together.

"It's an English name," Catherine boasts. "That is why you don't know it."

I smile at Catherine's tone. "Do not ever, ever call her *Caterina*," I tease. Although my tone is light, I remember that Catherine's heritage is serious to her, and she frequently reminds me that she had an English mother. How she can be so sure of this, I do not know.

"No, never," agrees Catherine, and she reaches out a hand to Monica. "I'm very pleased to know you, and I'll help take care of you."

Cecilia has already left the rehearsal hall. She must have known that I was no good for any more practice today. The three of us, however, need to put away our instruments and music.

"I understand that you are hungry. I am as well, but we have to go to vespers first," I tell Monica. "Before long you'll understand the routine of the *ospedale*. It is the bells, always the bells, telling us what to do."

I answer the call of the chimes by leading Monica to the sanctuary for evening prayers.

Over the next few days, Monica does indeed settle into our life at the *Pietá*, and the other girls, after initial surprise at her appearance, accept her presence. She shadows me throughout the day, and every time I play Speranza, I get the small cello for Monica to hold. I do believe she will learn a great deal by watching me, and I find that when she watches me play, I play with elegance.

My confidence in my playing grows, as does my ability. When I practice now, it's as if my hand learns what to do on its own: my head doesn't have to tell it. My hands now play the language of music without translation in my head. More than once, Don Vivaldi nods with approval in my direction at rehearsal. Cecilia also takes note of the strides I am making, and she tells me sincerely that I am getting very, very good. I will never admit this, of course, to Signora Priora, but I'm not suffering so much from her punishment after all.

On Saturday morning, Annamaria, Don Vivaldi's favorite violinist, approaches Monica after our rehearsal. She doesn't look straight at Monica's face, but she presses something into her hand and hurries away. Monica's face beams with happiness as she looks down at the small scrap of fabric wrapped around some candied nuts. "For me!" she exclaims.

"You can't eat them today because it's Lent," I tell her, adopting my role as teacher, "and you can't have sweets except on Sunday. But they'll make a fine treat for you to have after the concert tomorrow."

"I'll share with you and Cath—er—ine." She looks at Catherine with a mischievous expression. "Not *Caterina*," she adds, making our friend laugh.

We go to lunch together, and I notice that Monica pushes at her food and doesn't eat very much.

"Don't you like bean soup?" I ask.

Her little face is somewhat pale as she answers me. "It is good, so good, but I do not think I'm very hungry right now."

"The food will be better tomorrow," I say, "and then you'll be hungry."

"We eat like rich people here," she claims. "I have never before had so much food placed in front of me."

I have no response for this puzzling statement. I don't think rich people eat the coarse brown bread that we eat here. By the time I'm through eating, Monica has started gulping shallow breaths, something she has done a few times before.

"I'm going to practice some more this afternoon," I say, "but you should go rest for a while."

She offers no argument and nods. As we leave the refectory, I tell Signora Silvia that Monica doesn't feel well.

"Go on and practice," Signora Silvia assures me. "You need to be in top form for the concert tomorrow. I will take care of Monica. Don't worry a bit."

I leave Monica nestled against Signora Silvia's plump side, and I hurry back upstairs. To my delight, Cecilia is in the rehearsal hall.

Don Antonio Vivaldi is the music director of the *Ospedale della Pietá*, as well as the conductor of the orchestra and choir, but he gives lessons to only a select few. Most of us are instructed by older, more accomplished girls and women. When I was about nine, a couple of the older musicians determined that I had an aptitude worth nurturing, and my serious lessons began then. I didn't fully understand at the time that being chosen as a musician meant that I wouldn't have to scrub floors or slop chamber pots or take on any number of menial tasks, and I didn't understand that I would have meat when others might get only rice.

Cecilia wasn't my first teacher. She was only twelve or thirteen when I started playing, but she displayed remarkable talent as a cellist and took on the additional responsibilities of teaching when she was fifteen. I was one of her first students, and we've always worked well together.

In attitude, Cecilia is a stern and demanding teacher, but she is demonstrative with praise whenever praise is earned. In appearance, she is incomparable: she has a long, graceful neck and a knack for holding her head at just such a tilted angle so as to seem totally in control of her situation. Her cinnamon-colored hair shines with auburn highlights when struck by the sun, and it falls in long, luxuriant waves down her back when unrestrained. Most of the time, however, she keeps it plaited in a single, simple braid, and this style emphasizes the fine structure of her face—patrician angles rather than curves.

Perhaps I err when I say that it is her appearance that is so remarkable, because really it is her carriage that sets her apart as an extraordinary young woman in the midst of hundreds. She walks with her spine straight, her shoulders back, and her chin tilted up ever so slightly. When she sits to play her cello with her slim hands adroitly in place, the observer knows that she commands the instrument. Hundreds of aristocratic ladies have paraded before us in the concert audience, but I have never seen one who projects the poise and serenity that Cecilia bears. It is almost as if she is an aristocrat.

With my dull brown hair and pale green eyes, I am not homely, but I am not pretty either, and I see in Cecilia everything I long to be. If I lived in a real family, I would want Cecilia to be my big sister.

She says that I have made her proud because I have learned to play so well; she says that my talent reflects her instruction. Several months after she first started giving me lessons, Cecilia began referring to me as *Piccola Gatta.*

"Why do you call me Little Cat?" I asked one day after the lesson.

She smiled. "Because, like a feline, you seem to have something secretive, and perhaps a little mischievous, behind your green eyes."

This afternoon we play together, teacher and student, until the light fades around us. We know our parts, and we are ready for the concert tomorrow. The music of our cellos matching strength is a powerful wave coursing through the hall.

"You're playing so well that you're passing me by," she says, tucking a stray lock of hair behind her ear when we finish. "You're keeping a secret, but I think something is pushing you. I can tell that you're hiding something."

45

I wipe a droplet of perspiration off my forehead and can't restrain a broad smile. "I want something, Cecilia, I want something so much."

She looks at me with interest.

"I dream every day about Don Vivaldi letting me be the one to go to the front of the orchestra and play Speranza with the others behind me. I want him to choose me to play a solo in a concerto. "

She could laugh at me or discourage me, but it's too late to take back my words. Instead of scoffing, Cecilia nods her head. "It's within your grasp, Isabella—truly it is."

Her words delight me.

"I've never been chosen, as you know," she says, "but I don't think I have ever had the fever that burns in you. Yes, I do believe that someday very soon the *maestro* will write a concerto that features you and your Speranza."

With that subtle affirmation, I puff out my chest a little, because if Cecilia believes it, then it must be so.

"There is more I think," she says. "I have heard whispers that one night you and Catherine didn't sleep in your beds. I think that whatever happened that night has caused you to grit your teeth and practice like a demon, *si*?"

I bite my lower lip.

Cecilia shrugs her shoulders. "It is nothing, though. You don't have to confide in me if you don't want to."

I ponder this a moment. Catherine and I have tried to keep the events of that night private, but the secret spills forth. "It was the fireworks, Cecilia!"

Cecilia's head jerks sharply, and I can see that I have jarred her ever-serene composure. "The fireworks in the *Piazza San Marco*?"

"*Sì*," I say. "It was magical beyond description, but I'll try to tell you about that night if you want."

She recovers her poise and smiles furtively. "*Sì, Piccola Gatta*, I would very much like to hear of this adventure."

# Chapter Seven
## The Price of Adventure

Cecilia sits straight and folds her hands while I conjure the vision of the scene in the *Piazza*. I want her to share my feeling of being in that magical place, to remember every detail. And so I begin my tale for her.

*On that night, Catherine and I have done something we have never before done—we have left the Pietá alone and without permission. We are in search of the fireworks, and we are giddy with thrill and excitement as we fall in with the masqueraders streaming through the narrow streets. Jostled by the swarming crowd, we come to the side of the Basilica di San Marco, and then we are carried by the flow right into the Piazza itself. The incredible sight causes me to gasp in wonder.*

*Before us, a colorful multitude of people throngs the immense space of the Piazza San Marco, their movement like a rainbow-hued wave on the ocean—scarlet costumes, violet costumes, yellow, pink, and blue. Most people are wearing masks made of papier-mâché, especially the baùta, the black or white mask that covers just half the face. As I look around the square, a huge open space, I see mounted on the pillars of the buildings hundreds, maybe thousands of torches that illuminate the festivity. I see brilliant costumes swirling below and the torch flames flickering above.*

*Ruling over all, though, is the majesty of the Basilica di San Marco, and this beautiful structure rises from the ground with a splendor that is surely unrivaled in all the world. Even though I am helpless to resist the pull of the crowd, I try to count the number of*

49

*statues and crosses topping the spires and onion-shaped domes. Five huge arches grace the ornate building, and beneath each arch is a gilded mosaic. In the center mosaic, the largest, I see Jesus, Our Lord, in the presence of His saints and angels. But I am struck most by what is above the arches.*

*Four powerful bronze horses prance in majesty above the arches. Surely these beasts witness to the power of Venice!*

*Jostled among so many bodies, Catherine links her arm through mine to keep from being separated. I am holding fast to her when the torches are extinguished and a hush of anticipation falls on us. Catherine and I hold our breath in expectation because we have risked so much for this, and at last the spectacle begins.*

*A startling boom heralds the first shards of light that rocket into the black velvet sky. Up, up, up go the emerald-colored fireworks, and when the flashes of light are high above us, they fan out into a cascade of twinkles that dance above the Doge's Palace and then spiral down to nothingness. The next explosion produces a fountain of ruby red, then sapphire, then amethyst. The glittering jewels in the sky are more brilliant than any I have ever seen on the rich women who come to our concerts.*

*Boom! Boom! Boom! I love the thrill of the staccato beat sending stream after stream of dazzling light upward. I cover my ears, but I can't help smiling broadly. On and on it continues, and my chest vibrates with each pulsing boom. My heart races as rapid-fire explosions catapult a constant stream of multi-colored fireworks high above the crowd. The climax of jewel-colored crystals soars above us, and the sky is alive with dancing color.*

*On and on it goes until the fireworks above have encapsulated the whole world in their magic, and Catherine and I are part of it. I don't want this miracle ever to end, but at last it must. The glorious, radiant points in the night sky dissolve, abandoning all of us revelers to* darkness. *Stillness permeates the crowd because we are all awestruck by what we have seen. After several moments, the crowd erupts in wild cheers for the spectacle.*

*Catherine and I yell with abandon. There's a little girl beside me who squeals, and her mother indulgently beams at the little one's face and drops a kiss on the top of her head. Catherine follows my gaze to the mother and child, and Catherine smiles. But I do not.*

*Then one by one, the torches around the square are once again lit, and the darkness of the Piazza is chased away by the hundreds of glowing flames. The woman beside me clasps her daughter's shoulder and warns, "Stay close, mia cara, for I would not want to lose you."*

*The excited throng begins to move in all directions. I am so stunned by the marvel that I can hardly find my voice. Truly, I had to see this to understand the thrill. At last, I manage to croak out, "We should start back now."*

*Catherine nods, her face glowing. "Isabella, we saw the fireworks. We really, really saw them for ourselves!"*

*"Yes, we saw the fireworks." My face flushed, I turn to look directly at Catherine: "And it was worth the price!"*

I pause in my account of that evening. I want to tell Cecilia the rest of this tale, about the part that is terrifying and makes my heart race still, but the bells are pealing now and directing us to the next hour of our day. The rest of my story will have to wait. I exhale a deep breath and look at Cecilia.

She studies me with consideration. "Well, you mention a price," she says, "and I think I understand now. Has the responsibility for Monica been given to you as a form of punishment for breaking the rules that night?"

I nod. Cecilia pauses and then raises her eyebrows. "But you saw the fireworks, *Piccola Gatta*, something most of us have never seen. Indeed, I believe your adventure was worth the price."

# Chapter Eight
## *A Boy Named Niccolò*

Signora Silvia says that Monica is feeling so bad that she won't be able to come to the concert this afternoon. I love our Sunday afternoon performances, so I want Monica to watch me, but Signora Silvia says that Monica is still frail today and shall spend the day in the infirmary building up her strength. I want to argue, but I don't.

"Our little Monica went through a horrible ordeal with that fire, and she's never fully recovered," says Signora Silvia. "We're going to indulge her with rest and prayers so that her little body can regain its full strength. Signora Pellegrina will stay with her in the infirmary and take special care of her."

"So Signora Pellegrina won't be playing violin with us today?" I ask. Signora Pellegrina is a gifted healer, but she also plays with the orchestra on occasion. She is old now, and I think she's lived here forever.

Signora Silvia shakes her head. "Signora Pellegrina told Don Vivaldi that today she needs to be a nurse more than she needs to be a musician." Signora Silvia smiles and continues, "I don't think Don Vivaldi wanted to argue with her. One of these days he might need her special medicines."

I'm disappointed about Monica's absence from the concert, but I too want her to be fully well. I've discovered that when my young charge is shadowing me, I play better than ever. I am reluctant to admit it, but I think that showing off for her pushes me to the top of my form. I do believe, truly, that watching me play is a good way for Monica to begin appreciating what a fine instrument the cello is.

The oppressive clouds and mist have lifted, and a clear, clean sunlight washes our city and fills the church with a luminescent glow as we file into the choir loft. We all wear our pretty concert gowns, and I do think the white dresses make us look like angels.

Now that the season of *Carnevale* is over, there are not so many people in the city to come watch us, but those who do come want our music to take them to beautiful places beyond where they sit. I imagine that while we play, they will fly on the wings of the harmonies rising throughout the church, and their spirits will soar. At least that is the way I think of our music — powerful breezes of melodies that allow our listeners to glide among the clouds while they are yet seated.

Today, our music will be especially powerful, because Don Vivaldi has written a cantata for the day's program. All sixty of us, vocalists and instrumentalists, will be performing. As usual, the violins have the most prominent instrumental parts, but Catherine does have a brief solo on her oboe. My part is not so significant, but I am well prepared, and I know that the cellos will be flawless.

When I sit down, I look out over the audience before I begin tuning. I see several patrons who always come to see us, including several of the men on our board of governors with their wives. Signora Priora is in charge of us, but the governors are in charge of her. I also notice, seated on the third row, a family who has come at least twice before. My roving glance is stopped short by their son, a boy who looks just a few years older than I. He seems to have his eyes squarely on me. I quickly look down at the sheet of music before me, but I can't resist

54

looking back at him. He is indeed looking at me! I fight the impulse to avert my eyes a second time and now I keep my gaze boldly on him. His eyes connect with mine. He is, I believe, quite comfortable to look at, with thick wavy black hair and a smooth olive-toned complexion. From his manner of dress, I judge him to be in the wealthy merchant class. From this distance I cannot be sure, but I guess that his eyes are deep velvet brown.

"Niccolò Morelli." The whispered words break my stare as I abruptly glance to Cecilia at my side. "Niccolò Morelli," she repeats with her trademark half-smile. "His family is in the spice trade."

"How do you know about him?"

"Shh," she cautions, taking up her bow. "The *maestro*...."

Don Vivaldi, resplendent in his customary red concert jacket, steps forward, and the audience members shuffle their feet at the appearance of *Il Prete Rosso*, The Red Priest. He shakes the wayward strands of his white wig away from his face as he lifts his baton. He looks first at the instrumentalists, and I feel my heart swell in my chest when I lift my bow to touch Speranza's strings at the *maestro's* direction. The vibrations in Speranza's belly join the sounds made by Cecilia's cello and the other instruments, and the force seems to transport me beyond the walls of the *Pietà*. When the singers open their voices to ride the waves of music, an ethereal beauty fills the space like sunlight after a drenching rain.

Maddalena, one of the sopranos, sings an aria, and the hairs on my arm stand up as her voice rises into the heavens. As Maddalena retreats, Catherine comes in with her oboe solo, and it is flawless. The strings come in after Catherine, and my Speranza sings like a person, her voice as beautiful as Maddalena's. After three movements, we are done, and I feel as though the bliss filling my soul will force me to burst. The audience members blow their noses, wave their handkerchiefs, and shuffle their feet with gusto. Don Vivaldi singles out Maddalena, first, and then Catherine, for individual bows. We cellos have also played exceptionally well, and even though I feel half guilty for thinking it, my performance was stronger today than Cecilia's. As we prepare to leave the choir loft, Don Vivaldi nods toward me with unspoken approval.

I feel so good that he has noticed me that my feet barely touch the floor as I walk with Cecilia back to the rehearsal hall to put away our instruments. I gently nudge her in the side.

"So tell me what you know about him," I implore.

"Him, who?" she says as if she doesn't understand.

"You know who," I tell her. "That boy, the one you called Niccolò Morelli."

"You are interested in knowing more about him?" she teases.

"Perhaps," I acknowledge.

She nods at me, but before she can respond, we are interrupted by the arrival of Signor Coradini, a member of the board of governors that oversees the administration of the Ospedale della Pietá. I am somewhat taken aback as he approaches us with a nod of his head in greeting, but I recover my manners and drop to a deep curtsy, holding wide the heavy skirt of my white gown. "How do you do, Signor?"

Cecilia follows suit. I see now that Signora Priora and one of the other older women follow a couple of paces behind Signor Coradini, because of course he cannot come into our area unattended. Our virtue must always be protected. Signora Priora gives a slight nod of approval for our appropriate manners.

"I am well pleased, girls," he says warmly, "
extend an invitation to you both to come with me
reception and meet some of our patrons." He loo
and adds somewhat mysteriously, "I believe you have already
met some of them. And might I add, Cecilia, how proud I am of
you today. I always enjoy watching you play."

The reception. I have never been invited to one of the
receptions before, but I know that Cecilia has been included
several times. On any other day, I might have suffered from
insecurity, but today I have almost as much self-confidence as
Cecilia, so I enthusiastically agree. When I think to look past
Signor Coradini to Signora Priora, she nods assent. She calls over
Gabriella and Lucia to take our cellos from us, leaving us free to
go.

Signor Coradini is a fit man of medium height with a ruddy
complexion and reddish–brown hair a couple of shades lighter
than Cecilia's. He offers each of us an arm and gallantly escorts
us to the salon on the first floor of the *ospedale*, bustling with a
jovial crowd. I notice that when Signora Priora enters, she bows
respectfully before the richly dressed visitors. I know that
behavior in this room helps determine the level of financial
patronage that the *Pietá* will receive.

Signor Coradini strides through the room, and as I study the
people we pass, my heart beats faster. It thuds wildly in my
chest as we continue our course toward a small group standing
in front of a tall window overlooking the lagoon, a group that
includes that boy, Niccolò Morelli, and the couple I presume are
his parents.

"Greetings," says Signor Coradini as we approach, and the
group turns to us with interest. "The *Pietá* is honored to have
such distinguished visitors as you with us today."

"Cecilia, Isabella," he continues, "it is my privilege to introduce to you Signor and Signora Morelli, and their son, Niccolò."

All my training in etiquette is tested as I strive to remember the proper behavior in spite of the wild pounding in my chest. Once again, I hold wide my skirt and tuck my right leg behind my gently bended left in a curtsy that could almost pass for graceful. "I am most honored," I say demurely, extending my right hand. "Signor Morelli, Signora Morelli..." and then words fail me.

"Please call me Niccolò," he hastens to say, and he takes my hand and grasps it warmly. I look up at him and cannot help the slow flush of red heat that creeps up my neck and cheeks. I hate myself for showing embarrassment, yet I enjoy the introduction, the feeling of my hand briefly in his.

Signora Priora's attention has been diverted elsewhere, but Signora Silvia has materialized and discreetly stands watch next to the drapery panel behind Niccolò.

"I enjoyed your concert," he says. "You played very well."

"Thank you very much," I say. "I'm glad you were able to come. We worked very hard preparing for today."

He cocks his head. "You did? Is it much work being a musician?"

Surprised at the question, I forget my reticence and hasten to answer. "Indeed it is. Don Vivaldi conducts our rehearsals several times a week, but in addition to that, I go to lessons and practice at least two hours every day, sometimes more if I feel that I need to. And that is on top of my studies and my chores."

"That sounds like a heavy burden for a girl," he concedes.

"Oh, it would be a heavy burden for a boy, too," I say, and Signora Silvia raises her hand to hide a smile. "But my work is a pleasure for me," I add.

"It has been a pleasure meeting you today," he answers, "and I hope we'll have the opportunity to talk again."

My response is checked by my reluctance to give him the easy satisfaction of knowing that I hope to see him again as well. So I simply smile and say, "We'll certainly be giving many concerts during the Easter season."

At that, Signora Morelli, his mother, steps closer. "I agree wholeheartedly with my son that the concert today was a delight. I look forward to another one."

Signora Silvia's neck cranes forward, as she apparently strives to hear the woman's words. The words are kind, but Signora Morelli's hawkish gaze makes me uncomfortable. It reminds me just a little too much of the calculating way that Signora Priora sometimes looks at me, as though judging my worth.

After a round of stiffly mannered goodbyes, Signor Coradini escorts me a couple of paces over to where Cecilia stands. She is talking with several guests, one of whom cannot take his adoring gaze off her. No longer a center of attention, I can observe what's going on around me. First of all, Cecilia seems to have her own chaperone standing watch. Signora Marta, our Latin teacher, is positioned close to Cecilia's shoulder. Signora's stance is nonchalant, but I know she is on alert.

I look from Signora Marta to the rest of the group, and I see two elderly men with their wives and one younger man whom I take to be a son. Now I understand what is so clearly before me—this man cannot take his eyes off our Cecilia. He is enraptured by her, and—yes!—I mean to use such a strong word, for truly he seems unable to take his gaze from her, not even looking away when someone else speaks. I will admit that Cecilia beams right now with an exceptional beauty. Her white concert attire is just like mine, but her grace and posture make her dress elegant. Her cinnamon-colored hair is twisted up at the back of her head revealing the slender line of her long neck, and two stray tendrils graze her flushed cheeks.

"Cecilia, my dear," says one of the older women, "I am so glad that you were able to come visit with us again today because I am enjoying getting to know you."

At this, Cecilia's admirer grins broadly and adds, "I, as well, Signorina. I look forward to seeing you again." He takes her hand and holds it a fraction of a second too long, for Signora Marta swoops in and interrupts.

"Excuse me," she says, "but it is time for Cecilia and Isabella to take their leave now. Thank you all so much for visiting the *Pietá* today. We look forward to the pleasure of your company again."

With no time for second thoughts, Signora Marta clamps one hand on my shoulder and the other on Cecilia's and guides us away. I catch Niccolò Morelli's eye one last time before I am pushed out of the salon. I am bursting with curiosity, but I have to bite my tongue until Signora Marta has seen us to the stairwell and sends us up to the dormitories alone.

My skin prickles with curiosity as I assail my friend. "Well, Cecilia, can you tell me now? Can you tell me what you know about the Morellis?"

"I know that they are out shopping. They are looking to strike a good bargain."

"Shopping?" I am dumbfounded. "What are they bargaining for?"

She stops and looks at me with a condescending shake of her head. "Silly girl," she explains, "they are shopping for a wife."

# Chapter Nine
## *Good Wives*

I grasp the handrail to steady myself. "Me?" I croak.

Before Cecilia can answer, I remember with clarity something that Signora Priora said on that night when she apprehended Catherine and me sneaking back into the courtyard, and now her words have meaning they did not have then.

"Did you know," she had demanded, "that there are several marriage contracts under negotiation for some of the older girls? These marriages would be good for the girls and good for the *Pietá*. Do you know why respectable families come to our *ospedale* to find wives? Because our *ospedale* has a strong reputation for protecting the virtue of its girls, and this, THIS in your thoughtless selfishness, you have risked tonight."

Signora Priora's words sound again in my mind. On that night, I had no concern whatsoever for marriage contracts, but now I am forced to consider this possibility.

"Is it you?" Cecilia responds, her eyebrows raised. "I saw that Niccolò Morelli had eyes only for you."

"But get married? I can't imagine leaving the *Pietá*." I shake my head. "I can't imagine leaving the orchestra. I felt so sorry for Lorenza last month when she had to leave to get married. I heard her say she wouldn't play her oboe again."

Cecilia raises her chin and draws up her shoulders in a haughty manner. "You are a child," she says. In spite of her demeanor, her words are soft. "Lorenza did not have to leave. She had a choice to get married, and she took it. She probably lives in a *gran palazzo* on the canal and is learning to run a household while serving maids curtsy before her. And someday she will have a baby of her own."

I ponder this revelation while we go into the rehearsal hall. Several others are here, but Cecilia pulls me to a corner where we can continue speaking privately.

"Now, I need to tell you something—something very important," she says. "That man in the salon, Signor Carlo Santi..." She halts and brings her hand to her chest, and a smile she cannot restrain brightens her face. "Signor Santi will be my husband. We will marry two weeks after Easter."

"Marry! You are going to be married!" I am assaulted by a storm of emotions. "You have to get married and leave?"

"Oh, no, *Piccola Gatta*," she says. "You have not been listening to what I have said. I am not being forced into this marriage. I have made the choice to leave. Isabella, I want to get married. I want to have a family." She smiles softly and continues, "And you saw my intended—he is a fine man, no? And I want to be a mother some day."

I feel my spirit draining away from me. "Have *I* done something to push you away?"

At this, Cecilia puts her arms around me and draws me into a powerful embrace, more powerful than I have ever known. "Of course not, *Piccola Gatta*. You bring me great joy. You are the best student a teacher could ever wish for."

"But what about your cello, Cecilia? Will you be able to play your cello anymore?"

"I will perhaps be able to play within my own family," she explains, "but it will be part of the marriage contract that I can never again perform publicly after the wedding."

"Why not?"

"I do not think the *ospedale* wants the competition from musicians who are no longer earning money for it."

"Oh, Cecilia," I say mournfully. "How can you give it up? I know you feel it too—the thrill when we are playing for an audience, especially when we are all hitting the notes in perfect harmony."

"It is wonderful, the feeling of performing in our orchestra, and I feel incredibly lucky, yes lucky, to have had the experience, but it is not the life I want forever. The life I want forever is to be married and have babies of my own, and I have that chance now."

She steps back and grazes her thumb across my chin. "My Isabella, you are my *sorellina*, my little sister. I ask for your happiness for me."

I take her hands in mine and squeeze them. "I wish you all the happiness in the world."

"Thank you," she says. "I believe you are forgetting the good part. When I am gone, you will be first chair in the cello section."

I smile. "I would rather be second chair forever and keep you always in the orchestra."

"No, Isabella," she shakes her head. "Do not fool yourself. You want to be recognized as the best."

I remember my other concern. "But what about me...and Niccolò Morelli?"

Cecilia tilts her head to the side and ponders my question. "You are young still. I think that Signora Priora will want you to have time to grow up a little bit. Don't worry, *Piccola Gatta*— when the time comes, you will have a choice. That is the way of things here."

When I leave the hall, I am engulfed by confusion, and I need a few moments alone to clear my head. I slip down to the courtyard. It is too much to hope that the garden will be deserted, because in our *ospedale* with its several hundred people, there is no such thing as being truly alone. The evening is cool, but not unpleasantly so, and several others walk or sit among the trees. A forsythia bush is blooming next to my favorite bench, which is located in a remote corner of the garden, just inside the high wall. As I approach in the gathering darkness, I realize someone else is already there.

"Isabella," calls a soft voice. "Is that you? Please come join me." I am relieved that it's Signora Silvia.

"*Buonasera*, Signora. I apologize for the intrusion," I respond. "I don't mean to interrupt."

"No bother at all. I welcome your company." She pats the space next to her on the bench. "Come sit with me for a few moments."

Thankful for the invitation, I ease down beside her ample girth and without thinking, exhale a heavy sigh. For several moments we just sit, and I enjoy the silent camaraderie.

She speaks first. "You played very well this afternoon."

"Thank you," I respond with little enthusiasm.

Signora leans away from me so that she can see my face. "The Isabella I know would be more excited about such a superb performance."

"Yes, Signora."

"Isabella, my ears are just for you right now, if you want to talk."

I turn toward her face, almost invisible now in the darkness, and I know that her eyes will be shining with sincere warmth. I inwardly debate what I can say.

"Things are changing," I respond weakly.

She nods her head. "Yes, in life there is always change. Even so, it's quite natural to be afraid of what might happen. Did Cecilia tell you her news? Is that what's bothering you?"

"Yes," I say, recognizing that I am very afraid of what might happen. "I want what is very best for Cecilia, but I can't begin to imagine what it will be like without her here."

"It will be different," affirms Signora Silvia, "but we will all manage just fine, even though we will miss her very much. In fact, I think you will probably become the principal cellist, and you will have some important duties with teaching. From what I have seen, you've had a good start with Monica."

"I'll never be as good a teacher to Monica as Cecilia has been to me."

"You are not giving yourself enough credit, Isabella dal Cello. Time and experience will make you every bit as good as Cecilia."

I think of Monica sitting with me again for a lesson. "How is Monica doing?" I ask. "Is Signora Pellegrina making her feel better?"

"Oh, yes." Signora Silvia nods her head. "That Pellegrina, er…Signora Pellegrina, asked Monica how she survived the fire. And do you know what Monica told her? That it was lavender and honey—her auntie kept her face and throat coated with a concoction of lavender oil and honey. Not to be outdone, Pellegrina, er…Signora Pellegrina, has also mixed up some of the potion and is applying it to Monica's face and throat several times a day."

"So is the potion working?" I ask.

"Well, she is getting better, and she certainly smells good. I checked on her just a little while ago, and I want her to spend one more night in the infirmary." Signora Silvia shakes her head in wonder. "Monica has been through a horrible ordeal. It truly is miraculous that she survived the fire that killed the rest of her family. The lavender and honey might help her on the outside, but I think her little body was greatly injured on the inside in ways we cannot see."

Signora Silvia takes my hand and squeezes it gently. "Isabella, I know that sometimes you lack the proper respect for Signora Priora, but I promise you that she understands the workings of the orchestra far better than you can know. I believe very strongly that she did the right thing by agreeing to take in Monica. At the very heart of things, Signora Priora wants what is best for us all, and she truly believes that God has a special purpose for Monica here."

"Playing in our orchestra?" I ask.

"Perhaps," she says, "but perhaps something even more. Anyway, I want us all to do what we can to help Monica regain her strength. I think tomorrow she'll be able to return to your care, and I know you'll let her have a light duty."

"I'll watch over her," I say, and then I draw a deep breath. As I exhale, I admit softly, "It didn't seem like a good idea at first, but I think it's working out well for me to be Monica's teacher. But there's something else I've been thinking about."

"My ears are still yours."

"Do you know that Catherine always talks about her mother? It's really silly how she thinks she might come back and get her some day."

Signora Silvia seems to take great care choosing her words. "Isabella, I think you know that there have been a couple of instances when a mother has returned and claimed a child she left here, although it is not something we usually expect."

"But Catherine is old already, probably as old as I am," I protest. "If her mother has not wanted her by now, surely she would never want her."

Signora Silvia ponders this before replying, "Some people have a very hard time letting go of that which is most precious to them. I know that Catherine devotes a great deal of thought to her mother, but I haven't seen that her daily life is disrupted by thinking so."

I shrug. "Well, I think it's on her mind too much. Signora, do you remember when Catherine came to the *Pietá*? She says she can remember her mother singing to her."

Signora lifts her fingers pensively to her lips and then nods. "Yes, Isabella, I do remember. I remember because the details of her arrival were unique."

"You do remember? What happened?" I press.

Then Signora Silvia tells me the story of how one afternoon about twelve years earlier she had answered the massive front door to an unlikely visitor. Standing before her was an older Chinese man holding a pink-skinned chubby toddler with ringlets of golden blonde hair sticking out all over her head. With them was an English sailor who served as translator. The small-framed Chinese man, with his ebony black braid hanging down his back, explained that he had come from the English ship docked near the *Piazza*, and he begged the kind Signora for help.

He was servant to the ship's captain and the captain's wife, who had been on board this voyage. Two weeks earlier, the captain had contracted fever and died within four days. Three days ago, the captain's wife fell ill, and even though the ship's doctor was doing all he could to keep her comfortable, he had given up on her survival and expected her to die within the next day. Signora Silvia says that the servant shook his head with great sadness and explained that with the toddler's mother so gravely ill, there would be no one to care properly for the child. The ship had to meet its schedule and debark with the tide, and the Chinese man implored Signora Silvia to take the toddler, named Catherine, so that he could do his duty to his late employer by ensuring the safety of his young daughter.

Signora Priora had to make the decision, of course, and she hastily agreed with Signora Silvia that the *ospedale* should rescue the beautiful toddler.

"Well," Signora Silvia sighs deeply, "as she was handed to me, Catherine chattered with a big smile, calling me *Mamma, Mamma.*"

I am stunned into silence.

"I remember," Signora continues, "how the old man just shook his head and said to her, 'No Mamma.' He handed Catherine a silver rattle and turned and walked back toward the *Piazza.*" And she adds softly, "I think he was crying as he walked away."

A soft breeze rustles the branches of the pomegranate tree above us. I stare into the darkness.

"So that is the story of your friend's arrival," says Signora Silvia, "and I bet that rattle is stored safely somewhere in Signora Priora's office." And then she adds, "I have always called her Catherine, though others might have tried to rename her *Caterina*. I feel as if her real name is Catherine."

I am astonished by the tale of Catherine's arrival and the detail of Signora Silvia's memory, and I can hardly voice more than a whisper, "Do you remember when I came?"

She puts her plump arm around my shoulder. "I am so sorry, *mia cara*, but I do not remember for sure. You understand that so many baby girls and baby boys have been left, and I cannot remember all the circumstances."

My chin drops to my chest with profound disappointment. I am not worth remembering.

"But, Isabella," she adds, "Signora Priora has kept a record of information about all the babies who have been left at the *Pietá*."

# Chapter Ten
## Kneeling in Contrition

What would my life have been like if my best friend hadn't come to the *ospedale*? My first encounter with Catherine was so long ago that I can't remember it. She's always been there for me, my friend, my confidante. And now I hear this unusual story of her arrival, and I know why she insists on her English name. Does Catherine know this tale? Has Signora Silvia told her about it, or does Signora not think it worth telling? I don't ask. As the questions swirl through my head, Signora Silvia rises to leave, but she gives me permission to stay in the courtyard a while longer.

The memories of that night—the night we slipped out— push out all other thoughts in my head, and I remember what Catherine and I fought about. The night of the fireworks, Catherine and I had endured a terrifying threat on our way home. Signora Priora had apprehended us here in this same courtyard and sentenced us to a night kneeling in the church. Still sitting on the bench next to the wall, I close my eyes now and review in painful detail the rest of the events that happened that night—before I knew the truth about Catherine's story.

*"Follow me now," commands our jailer. "Quietly, so you do not disturb anyone else."*

*We fall in line behind Signora Priora as she pushes open the heavy wooden door leading from the courtyard back into the ospedale. In the dimly-lit hallway we unexpectedly encounter Signora Silvia. She stands holding a small bundle, and a weak mewling sound comes from*

73

the swaddled form. Signora Priora stops before Signora Silvia and briefly glances down. "Well, is it a boy or a girl?"

"I don't know. We brought it in just a few minutes ago," answers Signora Silvia, snuggling the infant. "I haven't unwrapped it yet. I was waiting for you."

"This will be a long night," says Signora Priora wearily, squeezing her eyes and rubbing her temples. "I have to take care of these two first."

Signora Silvia considers us curiously, but she is offered no explanation. Seeing the bundle in her arms, I recall that Catherine and I heard a bell as we were returning. It must have been the bell this baby's mother rang to alert the matrons to look in the scaffetta for another abandoned child.

"Go ahead and take care of it," instructs Signora Priora. "Bathe it, make sure it is warm, and take it to a wet nurse. We will have it baptized in the morning."

Signora then motions for us to follow her, but she turns to Signora Silvia and adds, "Please log the details after the child is taken care of. And remember to make note of any personal effects that you find with it."

We trail after Signora Priora through a narrow hallway, turn into the grand foyer of the ospedale, then pause before a massive door. Signora extracts a ring of keys from her deep pocket and adroitly finds the correct one to unfasten the lock.

We step into the church sanctuary, cold and dark. Before us a bank of candles burns and throws wavy shadows on the walls and statues. We approach the altar and genuflect. I am careful to keep my posture straight as I drop my right knee to the floor, bow before Our Lord, and make the sign of the cross. I inhale deeply the pungent scent of lingering incense.

"Kneel," Signora commands simply, and we do. "Remain here until I come for you in the morning. I will know if you try to sit or lie down."

And she turns and leaves. We hear her retreating footsteps on the marble floor, her light tread retracing her steps, then the sound, very faint, of the key in the lock. And she is gone.

We remain in silence, absorbing the enormity of all that has passed in the last few hours. The tears that threatened me earlier retreat in the face of the reality that all we have to do is kneel all night long. I am, first and foremost, a musician, trained in order, discipline, and conformity. Kneeling until the break of dawn will not break me—or Catherine.

"Do you believe in miracles?" I ask.

"I believed in miracles even before tonight," she answers. "But tonight I think we were saved by a miracle."

"Me, too." A few minutes pass, and I sense that Catherine is worrying about something. "I'm sorry she called you Caterina. I know you don't like being called that."

"I hate being called that!" she spews. "And she knows I hate it. She knows who I am. She knows that I am Catherine. I am Catherine! No matter what she does to me, she can't take away the fact that I had an English mother who gave me an English name." The growing anger in Catherine's tone is clear.

"It was a long time ago," I offer weakly.

"Not so long ago," she answers vehemently. "Maybe you have no memories, Isabella, but I do."

I am, I admit, jealous of her memories, so I say nothing. I just kneel and feel the cold hardness of marble beneath my knees. I lift my eyes to the sad face of Jesus on the crucifix, then look to the side altar at the statue of the Pietá—Mercy. It is a statue of Mother Mary holding her precious Son after he was brought down from the cross. I have *heard of a similar sculpture in the magnificent St. Peter's in Rome, and it was made by a great artist named Michelangelo. It is renowned for its breathtaking grace and beauty. But our statue is beautiful, too—at least it is to me. It might have been created by a lesser artist, but our Mary has an adoring face and loving arms that cradle her child with tender grief. Whenever I look at it, I feel a pang of unspeakable loss— mine more than Mary's.*

*"I had a mother who held me, too," whispers Catherine, sharing my gaze at the statue of the Pietá. "I remember that she hugged me, and kissed me, and even sang me silly songs with nonsense words. She loved me."*

*"You can't remember that," I hiss.*

*"Yes, I can," she calmly asserts. "Oh, I can't remember the words of the songs because they must have been in English, but I do remember the love of my mother."*

*"But can't you see," I argue, "that those memories have no meaning now? This is your life, here in the Pietá, playing music."*

*Catherine straightens her spine. "I don't care if you think I'm foolish, Isabella, but my memories do have meaning for me. I think she's still out there somewhere, and she'll come for me someday."*

*"Yes!" I cry. "I do think you're foolish. If you had a mother who loved you, you wouldn't be here in an ospedale. I am sensible, Catherine. I am not going to wish for a mother who didn't even care enough to keep me. My mother abandoned me, and I accept that. Like that baby Signora Silvia had tonight—how could its mother abandon it if she loved it? I know my mother didn't care for me, and your mother didn't care for you either!"*

*"I'm sorry for your bitterness, Isabella, but I don't share it. In fact, I'm going to offer up my night of prayer to ask God for another miracle—to help me find my mother."*

*"You are so childish," I scoff, feeling a painful desperation. Doesn't Catherine see that she doesn't need a mother? She has me—her best friend.*

*"You are my best friend, Isabella," she says, as though reading my thoughts, "but not a day goes by that I don't think about my mother and being reunited with her. I feel it here," and she points to her heart. "My feelings are so strong that I can't let them go."*

*"What you speak is silly make-believe. Mothers don't come to our door and ask to get their children back when they're as old as we are. They desert us, then they walk away and forget us. If they loved us at all, they would have found a way to keep us. If some woman came to the door and wanted me back, I wouldn't go with her."*

*"No, Isabella, you can't mean that. And even if you do, don't wish your feelings upon me because I do remember the love of my mother. True friends want what is best for the other, so you should be with me, not against me."*

*I am tired of disagreeing with her. She has talked like this before, and I have failed in my efforts to get her to see the error of her misguided hope. "Let me tell you what is best for me," I say. "I will offer up my night of prayer to ask God to let me be chosen by Don Vivaldi to play the solo in a cello concerto. I think I'll be good enough pretty soon."*

*"I will share your prayer," she says softly, "because I do want what is best for you. I'll do whatever I can to help you play in a concerto. I'll be there for you no matter what. Can't you say the same for me?"*

*I shake my head at her. "What you believe is stupid." And then a word comes to mind, a horrible word, and in frustration, I spit out the name she despises. "It's stupid, Caterina!"*

*She gasps sharply and grabs her belly as though wounded. "You are so hateful!" she cries. "Isabella dal Cello, what is it you want?" It is a question that I don't answer. She turns away and does not speak to me again.*

*The hours pass in silence as we each retreat into our personal hopes, maintaining with the self-discipline of trained musicians our rigid posture on the frigid February marble. The air grows colder, and I shiver, but I maintain my kneeling stance. A burning cramp spreads from my knees up to the front of my thighs, and radiates around to my lower back. My fingers and toes grow numb with cold. I try to remove myself from the pain by breathing deeply and retreating into my thoughts: Cecilia, Annamaria, Gabriella, Maddalena.... I picture them, and I do tell God that I am sorry for any action that might harm my friends at the ospedale, but I do not say that I am sorry for disobeying Signora Priora. That I will not say.*

*Most of all, I lift up a fervent supplication that a proud maestro will turn to me at the end of rehearsal someday soon, very soon, and say, "Isabella, you have played your cello as a virtuoso. I will write a cello concerto just for you, and you will play for all of Venice." And in my prayer, which now fades into delicious fantasy, I walk to the front of the girls' orchestra, beautiful in my white concert gown, my shiny brown hair adorned with a pomegranate blossom. I curtsy deeply, seat myself gracefully, and watch attentively as Don Vivaldi raises his arms. With my cello cradled between my calves, I raise my bow and play like an angel, with deep honey-warm notes sliding off the strings, floating across and through the audience. The men and women who hear me will smile in gratitude and nod their heads in appreciation. Speranza, my cello, is constant in my life. She will not abandon me, and I will never abandon her.*

*As shafts of sunlight filter into the sanctuary at dawn, I once again behold the statue of Mary holding Jesus. The soft morning light on her face illuminates a love that was pure and steadfast, one that was strengthened, not weakened, by hardship. Wasn't Mary just a young unmarried girl when the angel Gabriel told her she would have a baby? Mary didn't desert her baby, did she? But I was abandoned. I do not remember the love of a mother.*

Catherine does remember the love of a mother. That is the realization that I face when the bells ringing inside the *ospedale* intrude on my memories of that night in the church, that night before I knew the fantastic details of Catherine's arrival, and call me back to the present. Will I tell Catherine what Signora Silvia told me? She is my best friend, so I owe her the truth of what I know. But the truth can wait until tomorrow…or maybe even the day after that.

## Chapter Eleven
### Outside the Walls

A tantalizing hint of spring colors the air the next morning when Monica leaves the infirmary and joins me for our morning meal.

"You smell good," I tell her.

Monica makes the expression that I now recognize is her attempt to smile. "It's because of Signora Pellegrina," she says. "She took good care of me. Look at my face, Isabella. She kept a poultice of honey and lavender on it while I was in the infirmary."

I lean close. It does look smoother.

"You can touch it if you want to," she invites. I cautiously raise my fingers to her cheeks and graze the skin there.

"It does feel softer," I say.

"Softer out here," she says, pointing to her face, "but not softer in here." She inhales deeply, and I hear that her breath is ragged. Her appetite is better, though, and she eats a good breakfast. Afterwards, the two of us go upstairs to the rehearsal hall. I find my Speranza and get the smaller cello for my pupil.

"You know, Monica, you can give this cello a name if you want."

She seems to think about my suggestion while I adjust the strings on my bow, but before long, the magnet of spring lures us away from our lesson. After we carefully lay our instruments on their sides, we walk to the tall window where the brightness streams in. The dome of azure sky beyond our *ospedale* is endless, unmarked by even the barest wisp of a cloud, and the water—oh, the water of the lagoon is a shimmering sheet of turquoise, calm with the kiss of sunlight. This weather will be

81

good for whatever ails Monica, and the two of us stand in appreciation at the window and admire the lagoon.

"Isabella? Are you in here?" Signora Silvia's voice calls me with pleasant inquiry. With a heavy tread, she enters and spies us at the window. "Hmm," she remarks with a twinkle in her eyes. "I see that you are busy in prayer contemplating the goodness of God's glory on this beautiful day."

The giggle escapes me before I can stop it, and then Monica laughs too.

"Good morning, Signora Silvia," I say. "Thank you for your kind observation, but I think we're being lazy rather than prayerful."

"Do you now?" she asks with an exaggerated cock of her head. "But aren't you both looking out at the perfectly magnificent day and feeling a sense of gratitude that you exist in the midst of such splendor? If so, then I contend that you are being prayerful."

I nod in agreement. "I can't argue with you."

"And Monica is looking much stronger today," says Signora Silvia with satisfaction. "Monica, why don't you wait here for us? I need to speak with Isabella for a few minutes." On that note, she firmly grasps my upper arm and leads me back into the hallway.

"I need assistance today with a chore, and I thought you could perhaps help me." The words are serious, but I detect a playful undercurrent in her voice.

"I'll try to help in any way I can," I respond. "We don't have orchestra rehearsal this afternoon, but I certainly need to practice."

"Hmmm—I will need you for most of the day. Do you think you could delay your practice until after your evening meal?"

"Of course," I agree, curious about what I'm getting myself into.

"Good. And I think it would be beneficial if I asked Catherine to join us also."

"I'm sure she'll want to help, Signora, but what is it you need us to do?"

"I need to deliver an embroidered altar cloth to the monastery on San Giorgio. This is the first time that our good Benedictine brothers across the way have placed an order with the *Pietà*, so I want to deliver it personally. But I don't want to go alone."

"We are going over to the island of San Giorgio?" I squeal.

"Shh," Signora Silvia cautions, putting her finger to her lips. "This is not a holiday, but a serious job, and on that basis, Signora Priora has given me permission to take you and Catherine with me."

"I understand," I return, unable to hide the smile that is trying to split my face in two. I am going to cross the lagoon, leave my own island, something I have never before done in my entire life! Oh, I can see the island across the way with its bell tower rising above the dome of the church of San Giorgio Maggiore. It sits directly across the *Canale di San Marco* from our *ospedale*, and whenever I look out the window of our rehearsal hall, the rising spire of the *campanile* punctuates the view. And today, I will get to venture across the water to see first-hand what lies beyond.

Signora Silvia smiles indulgently and touches my shoulder. "Isabella, it's just a monastery we are going to."

"But it is somewhere, and it is not here."

"There will be just enough room in the gondola for one more—I was thinking about Monica. It is a perfectly pleasant day."

"Of course," I heartily agree, wishing I had mentioned the idea first. I skip down the stairs to look for Catherine, and I find her in our dormitory. When I tell her Signora Silvia's plan, she at first looks fearful. "We're going outside the walls and taking Monica?" she asks. "But what if something happens like it did that night? We can't let anything happen to Monica."

"We'll be with Signora Silvia," I assure her, but now I think about Monica's safety. I have had occasional nightmares since that night, and evidently Catherine was as shaken by the scare as I was. She and I look at each other, the shared secret in our eyes. We had left the *Piazza* San Marco and were reeling from the wonder of the fireworks we had just seen. We were jubilant, but events that night destroyed our carefree joy. I involuntarily close my eyes when the memories assail me.

*Walking away from the Piazza, I feel surprise when I am jostled from behind. What's happening? The bump feels deliberate! I draw closer to Catherine and link my arm in hers once again. She looks at me with a startled expression on her face. She's being pressed from the opposite side.*

*I look straight ahead and attempt to keep my pace steady and resolute. Catherine's gait matches mine. Remembering our way, we turn to the right and walk a short distance along the side of the canal. My heart begins to race because warning bells are clanging in my head. There are definitely others following us now! Without turning around, I try to figure out how many. I guess there are at least two behind us, perhaps three, and then we reach the alleyway where we need to turn left to get back to the Pietà. With the tall buildings and high walls on either side, the narrow street stretches as a dark, stygian tunnel, but we plunge into it. With rising panic, I hear the footsteps follow. I pull Catherine closer to my side and whisper, "It will be fine. We don't have much farther to go."*

*But the reassurance is barely out of my lips when one of the stalkers breaks from his pack and leaps with feline agility in front of us. I can't help the small scream that escapes my lips when I see the hideous mask he wears — that of a sinister cat, a cat from the depths of hell.*

*"Buonasera to you, Signorina," he says with an oily smooth greeting to me, and then he bows to Catherine. "A buonasera to you, too."*

*Trapped and unable to move forward, we stand rooted as two others join him. "Where are you headed this evening?" asks the one in a gaily painted white mask with a long, pointy nose. "Since you have no escorts, we will join you and offer you our protection."*

*"No, thank you," asserts Catherine. "We must get back to school right away, or someone will come looking for us."*

*At this, the three laugh in wry merriment. And then the one in the most frightening mask of all, the one that is simply solid black, covering his entire face, leans in close to me and says with slurred words, "You would have us believe you are schoolgirls? Schoolgirls who are allowed to go alone to Carnevale?"*

*I notice as he laughs again, this time in my face, that his breath stinks of old wine.*

*"We might look like fools," explains the cat face, "but we don't think like fools."*

*I fight to take shallow gulps of breath as a sense of alarm rises higher within me, but I stammer out, "So, you are from Venice?"*

"No, no," answers the one with the long nose. I can make out now that he is the tallest and bulkiest of the three. "We are students who have come from Padua to see what kind of Carnevale Venice puts on."

"That's right," agrees the one with the black mask, slapping his knees to emphasize his joke. "We are schoolboys, just like you are schoolgirls."

I think I hear a muffled sob from Catherine, but I try to focus on our predicament. The frivolous masquerade of pretending to be rich ladies is over. We really are just two brown mice, two cornered brown mice. The cat and his two cohorts are toying with us, predators teasing their prey. I think to buy some time. "Do you all go to university in Padua?" I ask. "Or are you tradesmen?"

"Why do you ask?" The one in black presses his face just inches from mine. I know he has eyes, of course, behind the almond-shaped slits in the mask, but in the darkness, I can't see them. The covering over his mouth distorts his voice, and he seems a ghostly specter when he adds, "As we said, we are just pretending to be schoolboys, just like you are pretending to be schoolgirls. Don't you like this game?"

The one with the exaggerated nose wedges closer. "Pull your hoods back so we can see your faces," he commands. At that, an arm from the cat snakes forward, and before Catherine can react, he jerks her hood away from her face. The three collectively gasp.

Venice is a crossroads of the world, a place where it is very common to see people of many colors and backgrounds. Nonetheless, it is quite uncommon to come across a woman who has such pale golden blonde hair, and even in the blackness of the alleyway, Catherine's hair seems to glow like a halo. After a moment of stunned silence, the one in black whoops deliriously, then has to steady himself before falling.

"Bellissima!" exclaims the cat, slowly nodding with an attitude that bodes an ominous threat. He strokes her fine, silky hair. Petrified,

*Catherine does not stir, does not move one muscle. "We have chosen good companions," he says, "to celebrate Carnevale with us."*

*My knees weaken as I remember a warning issued by Cecilia after something bad happened to two of the older girls who left the shelter of the ospedale to make a delivery and got lost. "Terrible things can happen," Cecilia said, "unspeakable things. There are some bad men who prowl for unprotected females on the outside, so you must always keep your guard." Cecilia would not tell me exactly what happened. Instead, she lowered her voice and repeated, "Unspeakable."*

*I shudder as the largest foe's shoulder presses against mine in an intimidating manner. Fear chills me to the very core of my being as I imagine what could happen to the two of us. A primitive instinct constricts my breathing and warns me that what began this afternoon as a silly game of adventure has turned into something chillingly dangerous. This is not a game I know how to play, so I don't know how to win. The consequence of losing won't be mine alone to suffer, but Catherine's as well, and I am responsible for her being here. Physically, I recognize we are no match for their strength. I am so scared I can hardly breathe. But I have to remain calm, think clearly, and use my brain to get us out of this trap; otherwise, the price to pay will be unspeakable.*

I shake the frightening memories from my head as I hear Signora Silvia calling our names from the hallway. "Just remember, Catherine," I say, "we did get away. We took care of ourselves, and we'll take care of Monica. We'll never let anything bad happen to her."

"Yes," she agrees. "I shouldn't be afraid to leave. You're the one who saved us that night, Isabella."

# Chapter Twelve
## *The Bell Tower*

Within a half hour, Signora Silvia, Catherine, Monica and I are on the gondola landing at the side of our *ospedale*. A door on the lower level of our building opens directly onto the compact dock on the *Rio della Pietá*, a smaller canal that emerges from the island to empty into the larger *Canale di San Marco*. Secured to one of the brightly painted red and white poles, a sleek black gondola rocks in the water. The gondolier, dressed in breeches and a striped shirt, steps out of the open boat to assist us. He is a smallish, older man, but his shoulder muscles are firm, and he securely grasps each of us by the arm as we gingerly step down into the swaying craft. Signora Silvia lets the three of us get in first, and when I am seated, she kneels down to hand me the precious packet with the hand-embroidered altar cloth that we are taking to the monks. Monica and I sit on a bench built into one side of the gondola, and Signora and Catherine face us from the other side. The water laps against the dock.

After removing the ropes, the gondolier takes his place near the stern of the vessel, and with his long oar, he adroitly guides us away from the landing toward the open water. As soon as the gondola is in motion, the gondolier starts singing. The smaller canal empties into the larger one, and we pass beneath the arched stone bridge that crosses the *Rio della Pietá*. Impulsively, I wave at the few people who stand above us on the bridge.

What a sight we must be—one matron in her charcoal grey dress accompanied by three orphan girls in dull maroon dresses. One of the ladies above pokes her companion and points at us, and then both lean out for a closer look as our craft glides away. Their actions mean little to me until I see at my side that Monica has shrunk into her seat and lowered her head so that her face is not visible. Yes, of course I remember my first reaction when I saw her scars, but today I will not let her past tragedy overshadow our present adventure.

"Look, Monica, look," I urge, pointing to the *campanile* rising ever taller as we approach the island. "A dove on top of that spire could see the whole world." We can also see the imposing dome of the church on the island, and in the busy waterway that we travel, a score of watercraft ply the lagoon. Monica's head remains bowed. "Look at the ships, Monica. Look at the sailors, look at the buildings, look at the gulls!" I add with fervor, perching myself on the edge of the gondola seat. "Look at everything that is not walled in by the walls of the *Pietà*!"

Signora Silvia and Catherine laugh at my exaggerated enthusiasm, but still Monica keeps her eyes downcast. "And Monica," says Signora Silvia, "look at the elephants!"

The elephants? Catherine and I both whip our heads around, and Monica jerks her head up in search of the lumbering giants that we know only from books.

"Just teasing you," says Signora with a big grin, "but I really have seen elephants before."

Monica starts to giggle. "I've heard of elephants, but I've never seen them."

Catherine and I both shake our heads, admitting that we have never seen them either.

"Okay," says Signora Silvia, "I don't think I will be able to show you elephants on San Giorgio, but maybe I can show you the whole world."

Our gondolier with the rich voice docks our little vessel at Campo San Giorgio, the square, and helps each of us onto the landing right outside the impressive steps and entrance to the grand church. Signora Silvia smoothes her dress into place, adjusts her lace-edged white cap, and proudly clutching the precious packet with the altar cloth, walks toward the left side of the building. Monica falls in behind her, but Catherine pulls me back.

"What kind of secret past do you think she has," whispers my friend, "that she's seen elephants?"

We forget the mystery as we are admitted into the cool, dark recesses of the monastery, and Signora delivers the treasure. The young Benedictine monk looks us over with an expression that borders on admiration and asks, "Do any of you play in Don Vivaldi's orchestra?" Signora answers that I am a cellist; Catherine, an oboist; and Monica, a student of the cello. Brother Pietro, as he has introduced himself, nods appreciatively. "You all must be very, very good, because I have heard one of the concerts, and it was magnificent. And you," he says, turning toward Monica, "must show great promise as a musician. I wish you the best in your studies." He holds her gaze, and I get the idea that it takes great strength of will on his part to tamp down the urge to flinch and look away. Monica's lips curve into a crooked smile.

Signora calls Brother Pietro away from us and speaks to him in hushed tones. He shakes his head and answers in a voice louder than hers: "I do not think it is allowed."

Signora Silvia steps back from him, folds her hands together in front of her full chest and smiles beatifically, as though calling down the aid of the Holy Spirit. "It surely should be allowed," she counters, "for those who went to such trouble today to bring this altar cloth to you, an altar cloth that will help your monastery glorify God."

Brother Pietro opens his mouth for a final protest, pauses, and then admits defeat with a gesture of raising his hands. "Okay," he says, "I will get the key, but God forgive me."

"There is no need for forgiveness, I am sure," Signora answers serenely.

In a short time, we all stand at the door at the base of the *campanile*, the bell tower, while Brother Pietro inserts the long iron key into the lock. "Don't be long," he says, stepping back from the open door and motioning us in, "and be very careful."

"We will only be as long as it takes to see the whole world," answers Signora Silvia.

When we step inside, I tilt my head very, very far back and look up the staircase that winds up and up the square walls of the tower. I guess there to be well over a hundred steps to the top. Catherine and I climb the most quickly. Signora Silvia moves more slowly because of her size, and Monica starts to have difficulty breathing after only a few steps. After only two flights she stops and says in a raspy voice that she can climb no farther. I turn and go back down several steps to her and take her by the shoulders.

"You can do it," I encourage. "It's probably the only chance we will ever have to see the whole world, and I don't want you to miss it. I can help you."

I put my arms around her slender waist to lend her support and start back up with her. Her tiny, shallow breaths come more and more rapidly, and we stop to rest every few moments.

Signora Silvia draws a deep breath, "Monica, you do not have to go on. I will go back down with you."

Monica lets her head droop for a split second, then looks longingly upward. "I want," she declares in a voice barely there, "to see the whole world."

And so at last, after extraordinary effort on Monica's behalf, we reach the final step at the top of the *campanile* of San Giorgio Maggiore. Signora motions to Catherine to go on outside to the balcony that encircles the bell tower. When she opens the door to the outside, we are greeted with a clean luminescent glow of sunlight and a soft steady breeze. I gently push Monica out to the deck behind Catherine, and I follow, with Signora Silvia behind me.

What can I say? I have lived my life in a walled compound with few opportunities to venture forth, and now I stand with the whole world stretching away in all directions before me. I gasp in astonishment, and when I do, my nose discovers a wonderful surprise. "Smell!" I exclaim to the others. Puzzled, Catherine wrinkles her nose and looks at me blankly. Monica steadies herself as she leans against the half wall and says in a tiny voice, "I don't smell anything."

"Exactly," I agree. "I don't smell dead fish, I don't smell rotting vegetables, I don't smell human sweat." I close my eyes in wonder and draw a deep breath all the way to the pit of my stomach, savoring the purity of the air way up here.

We make a circuit of the spire, walking all the way around the landing, enraptured by the vista. Several seagulls soar and dip close enough that I can see the black tips on their wings. Up, up, up they go. Then they glide on the current across the shimmering water.

"Look at those seagulls," I say. "They are so lucky. They can go anywhere they want."

Signora Silvia snorts. "They are always hungry and looking for food. Does that sound lucky to you?"

I see across the lagoon, as though in miniature, our church of *Santa Maria della Pietà*, jutting out from the four-story building that is our *ospedale*. To the left of the *ospedale* are several buildings on the waterfront, and then the Doge's Palace. To the side of that, the two granite columns mark the entry from the lagoon to the *Piazza San Marco*. Tiny human figures, like busy insects, scurry along the quay.

The pigments of the architecture in Venice are rich and earthy—deep ochre red, golden sand, fleshy pink—topped with tiles of terra cotta. Defining the city are the numerous bell towers and spires that rise above the canals. Framing the scene of the city is the grayish-blue sky above and the deeper blue green of the placid water below. I have heard our city referred to before as *La Serenissima*, and today it certainly has the look of "The Serene One."

Monica is not looking at Venice. She has walked to the northwest corner of the tower and strains to see beyond the city to the mainland. Catherine approaches her and points to the distance. "I am from England," she says, "and England is somewhere that way, but much, much too far away to see. You would have to cross Europe to get there." She sighs wistfully. "I hope I get to see England someday."

I catch my breath, thinking of the tale of how Catherine came to the *Ospedale della Pietà*. I should tell her...but not today. I'll tell her another day.

After several moments' pause, Monica offers, "I think my home was that way." She gestures toward the west, beyond the islands of Venice. "My family had a vineyard. From the very first that I can remember, I helped pick the grapes."

Signora Silvia now joins us. "Perhaps when you are grown, you will get to return to the vineyards. That life must be in your blood."

"Oh, no, Signora. I want to be a nun. It is what I have always wanted."

I point out to Monica that she could be a nun who plays the cello.

Catherine laughs and adds, "Like Don Vivaldi—he is a priest, but he is our music director and a magnificent violinist."

"Is it really true then, that Don Vivaldi is a priest?" asks Monica. "I heard he never says Mass."

"He doesn't," I affirm, as we venture into a subject that I find very curious. "Signora, why do you think Don Vivaldi would choose to become a priest when his true calling seems to be for his music?"

Signora Silvia looks away with a hint of melancholy before she answers. "Choose? Maybe he didn't get to choose. Perhaps for his family the path to the priesthood was the path that offered him an education and musical training."

I start to respond, but before I can get a word out, she holds up her hand to silence me. "Please don't misunderstand me," she explains. "I don't mean that he isn't passionate about his love for God. But he honors and glorifies God every day with the beautiful music that inspires all of us."

I look at Signora Silvia and see that her eyes are moist. "Signora," I ask with a solemn whisper, "did you choose to come to the *Pietà*? Or have you been there forever?"

She weighs her response carefully before speaking. "Yes, I did make that choice—eventually. Sometimes life offers a profound choice, and you have some control of your future course. But at other times life forces you in a particular direction, and your feet must tread the only path before them. Either that or you just give up." She looks at each of us in turn and manages a wan smile. "Sometimes," she continues, "even though your heart is broken, you just have to make your feet move, one after the other."

We make one last circle around the landing before descending, delighting in the whole world before us. Before she enters the stairwell, Signora Silvia touches her heart and then blows a kiss toward the mainland. As we retreat down the steep steps, I grasp Monica's arm to steady her. By the time we reach the bottom, her chest is heaving with exertion, and she falls gratefully into her seat in the gondola. A chill breeze is beginning to blow across the water, and Monica pulls on her cloak as she looks around with curious interest. We cross the big lagoon, and her breathing grows steady.

"Signora," I ask, "what about the elephants?"

"Ah, yes, the elephants." Signora's gaze is drawn toward the mainland. "Well, that is a story for another day."

Monica follows Signora's gaze, but her attention is captured by a diving sea gull. As the sun strikes ribbons of light on the water, Monica squints against the brightness. In silence, we enjoy the return crossing, and I marvel at the peaks of the waves sparkling like diamonds. When we near the arched bridge that marks the entrance to the small canal next to our *ospedale*, Monica pulls her hood tight around her face and bows her head.

As the gondolier moors our craft to the striped pole, Signora Silvia speaks. "This has been a very special day for me. I feel as though I have had the joy of spending this day with my three daughters."

I am wonderfully weary after our excursion and more than a little intrigued. "Catherine," I whisper, linking my arm in my friend's as we walk toward home, "I think Signora Silvia has secrets."

# Chapter Thirteen
## *Escape*

Secrets—Catherine and I have secrets of our own from that night of the fireworks that only Signora Priora knows about. Sometimes I dream about the masked men who had us trapped, and when I wake up in a cold sweat, I have to remember in detail what really happened before my heart will stop pounding. Tonight the nightmare paralyzes me with fear as I lie motionless between Monica and Gabriella. I breathe deeply to steady my heart, and I make myself go over every detail of the incident so that I will know I am safe.

*"Stop it, you three," I assert with bravado. "Stop trying to scare her. This is Carnevale, after all, and everyone is supposed to have fun."*

*"Yes," agrees the cat, "we just want to have fun." He fingers Catherine's hair, I think mostly to defy me.*

*"Let's move along now," says the one with the pointed nose, "so we can find a party." He clamps one of his beefy hands around my upper arm. His slimy touch repulses me, but with great force of will, I do not recoil. I do not want to provide further antagonism. Somewhere deep, deep in my head I can feel an idea trying to surface, an idea prompted by his desire to go find a party. Once again I concentrate on the act of breathing in order to clear my mind so I can solidify the plan taking shape.*

*"But you are not from Venice," I say. "Do you know where to find a party?"*

*The one who reminds me of a specter, the one with the full black mask, speaks with halting words. "We hear there are parties everywhere. Venice has parties all over the place during Carne...Carnevale."* He steps away and makes a grand sweeping gesture, but totters and has to straighten himself up.

*"I would like to go now and find some spirits,"* he demands. *"Let's go. And the two of you are going with us."*

He seems to be having trouble forming his thought, and he certainly doesn't need any more spirits or wine, but it becomes crystal clear to me that his condition can work to our benefit. He is the most inebriated of the three, but I suspect his cohorts have also had a generous amount of wine this evening.

Now I have it! Every time I breathe deeply, I suck in the dank, overripe odor of the canal, but now the musty stench inspires me with a plan—the canal itself might help us escape! *"I have an idea,"* I say boldly. I look to my best friend and try to convey some sense of assurance to her. *"I have an idea about a party."*

It's too dark to see the expression in her eyes, but Catherine tilts her head in interest and straightens her shoulders somewhat. I inhale deeply, and then hum the same five notes in the minor key that I played on my cello earlier this afternoon. I am thankful when she echoes the notes back to me. It's a tiny gesture, almost meaningless, but it helps restore our wits. We may be threatened, but we have power in our partnership.

*"What's that song you're singing?"* demands the cat.

*"It's a melody,"* I correct him, *"a secret melody that is associated with a secret party."*

*"Oh, yes,"* exclaims the black-masked figure, *"you will tell us about the secret party. It must be a very good party indeed."*

*"Oh, yes,"* I agree, *"and you can only get in with our help, because it is part of a..."* and I lower my voice to a whisper, *"...a secret society."* And I embark on a ludicrous tale about a notoriously secret party that Catherine and I know how to get into.

*As I babble on, adrenaline feeding my lie, Catherine seems to shake off her paralysis and join my theatrical ruse. She manages to laugh ever so charmingly and say, "Family connections. Most simply, you can't know the society or get into the party without family connections, and we have those family connections."*

*"Then take us to the secret party," demands the black-masked one. "You can get us in, sì?"*

*"They're playing us for fools," exclaims the cat. "They don't know anything about a secret society!"*

*"They wouldn't lie to us," argues the man with the pointed-nose mask, moving slightly away from me. "I want to go to their secret party. It sounds more exciting than anything else we've done in Venice."*

*"You're a fool," says the cat. "You are both fools if you believe these silly girls." And the evil cat—the Devil's own demon, I think— reaches to grab the hood of Catherine's cloak.*

*"Stop it!" cries Catherine, jerking away from him. "We won't take any of you ruffians to the party if you keep acting mean."*

*"Leave her alone now," says the black-masked one, stumbling to push the cat away from Catherine. "We want to go to the party. Don't ruin it for us."*

*The cat draws back his arm, but the bigger man, the one with the pointed nose, checks him before he can punch anyone. He stares down at his cat companion. "If you don't want to go with us, that's fine, but we are going to the secret party with these girls. Maybe you should leave us now."*

*The cat pulls his arm from the other's grip and shakes his head. "You are both idiots." He wags his finger at me and Catherine. "And the two of you are conniving liars."*

*The cat turns in anger and with his face away from us, pulls off his feline mask and throws it to the street. He stalks away toward the Piazza, and I never see what the man really looks like.*

*My hand covers a sigh of relief escaping my mouth. The cat is gone. The sinister one who knows our game has turned and walked away. My eyes seek Catherine's in the dark. Again, I can't see her expression, but I can feel her relief there in the narrow alleyway. With just a little more time, we can carry our charade to its conclusion.*

*"I'm glad he's gone," says the one with the pointed nose. "Now, there are two of you and two of us." He traces his finger down my cheek. I swallow hard, but maintain my charade.*

*"But first we must get to the party," I say, stepping backward. "There's a ritual you must follow. You'll think part of it sounds silly, but you have to do it anyway."*

*"Then tell us already," says the man in the solid black mask. "We've had enough, 'nuff, 'nuff talk about it."*

*"We might as well continue down the alleyway," says Catherine, "right, Isabella?"*

*We walk into the utter darkness of the tunnel-like lane we entered earlier. I yearn for the comfort of walking next to my friend, but the big one has wedged himself between me and Catherine, and the pointed-nose one is firmly entrenched on my other side. He puts an arm around my shoulder, and fear makes my knees go weak. I force myself to stay alert and keep walking as he pulls my body to his. I cannot faint!*

*I focus on continuing our trickery because it's the only way Catherine and I can escape unharmed. While processing this truth, I try very, very hard to remember all the details of the dark lane leading to the Rio dei Greci, the small canal where Catherine almost tumbled into the water earlier.*

*"Have you ever been part of a secret ritual before?" Catherine asks the men. "It's like a game, you know."*

"And it doesn't always make sense to you," I add, "the things you have to do as part of the ritual, but you just remind yourself that once you get in, you'll have fine food and plenty of wine."

"You'll see plenty of pretty girls, too," says Catherine.

"You girls are pretty," says the pointed-nose one, squeezing my shoulder with emphasis.

"Not nearly as pretty as the other girls who will be at the party," I assure him.

We come to the end of this path and turn right. The next juncture on our right will be the lane leading to the Rio dei Greci, the small canal that's now key to our escape.

"My cousin Antonio whispered to me this morning that the ritual in effect tonight would be the Rio dei Greci ritual. You remember it, Catherine, don't you?" I ask.

"I...I...I am not sure I do," stammers Catherine.

"It's so clear," I say with a wave of my hand. "We talked about it earlier this evening, when we were on our way to the Piazza."

Catherine tries to play along, but this time she's not reading my thoughts. "I'm sure I do remember, but you're much better at explaining all the details. You go ahead and tell our friends about it."

I nod my head. "Okay. We're almost there." I pause in the street, and the pointed-nose foe releases me. "This is what you'll need to do." The two men look at me. I squint in concentration as I try to recall the number of doorways on the right-hand side of the alleyway that leads to the small canal. Are there three...or four?

"Well, out with it," impatiently demands the black-masked one. "We're ready for more wine. What do we all have to do?"

"We can't all get in together at the same time," I explain. "You two will have to go first."

"Oh, no," says the pointed-nose one, reclaiming his grip on my arm. "We stay together."

"But it's not like that in Venice." I shake my head and try to pull away from his grasp. "Men always go first. Surely, it is the same in Padua. We are just girls."

"It's like that in Padua too," agrees the black-masked one. "Men always go first there."

"And it's part of the ritual," adds Catherine. "If we don't follow the rules, the door will stay closed to us, and we will never get into the party."

"All right, then, all right," says the big one. "What do we need to do?"

I peer to the right, down the darkness of the alleyway that leads to the Rio dei Greci, and I make one last calculation. Four doors, I think— I'm pretty sure there are four doors. "You'll go this way," I direct. "You must hum the melody you heard us sing earlier." As if on cue, Catherine starts humming.

"You both try it now," she says. After a few attempts, they are able to echo the song quite accurately, and I worry that they might no longer be drunk enough to fall for this trick.

"You'll have to feel your way down the alleyway because it's so dark," I explain. "Every door should have a bronze knocker. When you've counted four doors, you'll knock four times, quite rapidly, then say together that you've come in the name of the Pietá. Then…"

"It's so dark though," protests the one in the black mask. "I can hardly see anything. How can there be a big party when it's so dark?"

"Oh, once the right door has opened, you'll see a festivity full of light," assures Catherine. "But you must listen carefully and make sure you understand exactly what to do. If you don't follow the details exactly, the doorman won't let you in, and won't let us in either."

"We're listening," grunts the one with the pointed nose. "Go on, now, and tell us the rest."

*I review the steps given so far and continue. "After you've knocked on the fourth door and proclaimed you've come in the name of the Pietá, you'll then proceed together, side by side, shoulder to shoulder, to the fifth door, and that one will open to you. Even if you hear someone approaching the fourth door, don't stop—you must continue rapidly to the fifth door."*

*"It's all part of the ritual," affirms Catherine. "The timing matters, and it's very, very important that you make haste in getting to the fifth door."*

*The black-masked one sounds suspicious as he asks, "What about you two? How do you get in the fifth door?"*

*"We have to repeat your ritual, after you get in." I shrug my shoulders. "That's how it is in Venice. We are not your equals."*

*The suspicion turns to humor as he laughs at my assertion. "Not our equals, eh? Girls could never be our equals!" He lightly hits me with a flat hand on the side of my head, and my ear smarts from the blow. Oh, God, I lift up a silent prayer, we must get away! They will easily overpower us if they decide to do so.*

*With a shaky voice, I ask the two men to repeat our instructions, step by step. I am satisfied that they understand the ritual exactly. This will work or it won't, but the time is now. With great force of will, I resume my hoax and playfully push the pointed-nose one in the direction of the Rio dei Greci. "Go on then," I urge, "and save some fun for us. We'll be just one minute behind you."*

*As they start hesitantly into the impenetrable darkness, I reach out and clasp Catherine's hand. I can feel that we're both holding our breath. We should run, but we don't yet move. Instead, we stand there listening to the spooky sound of the minor melody they hum as they count down four doors. I tighten my grip as I hear them call out in slurred unison that they come in the name of the Pietá. Can we run yet? Are they far enough away? Their footsteps recede rapidly as they head with blind optimism toward the canal just beyond the fourth door. I will myself into action, turn, and pull Catherine with me. We hear the splash and surprised cry of two bodies stumbling into the small murky canal, and we wait no longer! We leave behind the mustiness of the water and run with all the speed we can gather toward the haven of our Pietá.*

Yes, tonight I am safe. I am wedged between Gabriella and Monica in our bed, not wedged between two drunken men who could bring unspeakable harm to me and Catherine. My nightmare is simply that—a dream that terrifies me. Before I fall back to sleep, I grit my teeth and pledge never to let anyone terrify Monica as the cat and his cohorts terrified Catherine and me that night.

# Chapter Fourteen
## *The Cello's Song*

My nightmares subside in time because I'm always so sleepy when I fall into bed. Monica and I work, and we work hard, and I am happy at the end of the day. Over the next couple of weeks, we meet every day except Sunday in the fourth floor rehearsal hall and spend at least an hour, usually two, together. By the end of the lesson, Monica is always drained of energy and weak of breath, but she never complains or asks to stop. On the contrary, she approaches the cello with an enthusiasm I know only two other cellists in the orchestra to have ever had. Monica will practice a few simple notes over and over until she gets them right. She is not becoming a virtuoso overnight—that is not the case. But she brings to her musical training a passion that I share, and one that Cecilia showed before she decided to get married.

"I have something for you," I tell Monica one day when we are done playing. "Close your eyes and feel what it is." She lays her small cello on its side as I have instructed her to do, and she sits with her hands outstretched. Her misshapen mouth forms its half smile.

I reach into the leather case that holds my Speranza, and I withdraw a new red silk cloth identical to my older, faded one. I bartered to obtain this treasure. I am allotted two pieces of fish each Monday at supper because I am a musician, but Angelica gets only one because she is just a seamstress. Angelica likes to eat, so I have promised Angelica my second piece of fish for the next eight Mondays. In return, she has brought me this treasure from the sewing workroom.

"Keep your eyes closed," I tell Monica as I brush the cloth over her cheek.

"Soft," she says, nodding her head. I place the square of red silk in her open hands.

"Yours," I say, "you can look now."

"My own?" she squeals, stroking the smooth fabric.

"Now you can always take good care of your cello. Wipe down the strings and body every time you play."

She hugs the silk to her chest. "*Grazie*, Isabella," she says. "And Felicità."

"What?" I tilt my head. I don't understand.

"I am naming my cello *Felicità*," she explains. "Remember, you told me I could give my cello a name, just like you named yours Speranza." Her grey eyes twinkle.

By Holy Week, Monica learns and absorbs the rudimentary skills to play five simple notes fairly well, and then very well. She and I sit with our backs to the door playing an étude repeatedly and do not hear the approach of footsteps.

"Brava," comes the quiet, deliberate word. Don Vivaldi steps in front of us and nods appreciatively at Monica. "You are making excellent progress. Maria, is it?"

"Monica, Sir," she replies.

"Monica," he says slowly, as though considering his next words. "I don't just mean that you're technically right." He smiles broadly. "Anybody can be taught to run a bow over some strings, but you…you bring a beautiful voice to your music. You make the cello sing."

My heart swells with an unknown pride at that moment when I hear our music director's praise for my student. My student came into our *ospedale* a mere five weeks ago with no voice at all, no emotion, but since her arrival she has transformed into a happy, confident girl. She is still disfigured, of course, but the others in our community are used to her now, accept her, and no longer take note of her scarred face. Now she is the new girl learning to play the cello and not the new girl who was injured in the fire. She is Monica who smiles in her own fashion and Monica whose eyes dance with happiness.

Don Vivaldi taps his chest and asks, "Monica, are you winded? Are you having trouble breathing?"

A shadow falls across her face. "Yes, Sir, but I try as hard as I can not to let it bother my practice."

"You know, don't you, that I too have a breathing affliction?"

Monica's eyes widen in shock. "No, Sir, I didn't know that."

Don Vivaldi nods in my direction. "Isabella can tell you. She has seen me leave rehearsals because I could hardly breathe."

This is true. I've also heard the tale that one reason Don Vivaldi never says Mass anymore is because he can't stay on the altar for the whole time without having an attack of breathlessness. On the other hand, in my experience, he never suffers this problem while conducting a concert for an audience. When he performs in front of a crowd, he does so with energy and flair, quite the entertainer with his brilliant red hair and scarlet-colored livery, his special concert suit. People call him *Il Prete Rosso*—The Red Priest.

"You were in a fire, yes?" Don Vivaldi asks. "Your problems are probably because of the smoke you breathed," he theorizes, "but the tightness in my chest has always been with me, as far back as I can remember. But as far back as I can remember, I wanted to play the violin, and so I did. This breathing problem didn't keep me from excellence; and so it shall be for you."

He looks at me with satisfaction. "And you *Maestra* Isabella," he says, honoring me with the title given to the female teachers, "you are a good teacher. Is there anything more you yourself can learn? Do you want to begin studying with me?"

"Oh, yes, Don Vivaldi, more than anything!"

"Well, carry on here. You and I will work out a schedule later. Keep up the good progress, Monica." He turns to go, but as he exits the room, a sudden thought makes me hurry after him.

"Excuse me," I call out in the hallway. "Don Vivaldi, forgive me, please, but I have a request."

He cocks his head in interest.

I glance over my shoulder at Monica still sitting in her chair with her Felicità. She is looking at it and not at me. I share with him my half-formed idea that he might give permission for Monica to sit in the cello section of the orchestra at the Holy Thursday service. I think this might give Monica a hint of the thrill of being part of the music that will swell the church.

He pauses before answering. "Let me think on it," is all he says.

Later I catch Catherine going down the stairs, and I link my arm in hers. "He wants me to study with him," I whisper.

"Oh, that's wonderful," she says. "It won't be long now, Isabella. I bet he'll choose you for a solo pretty soon."

The rest of our day passes with routine precision, and Cecilia entertains everyone at the dinner table with her plans for the wedding. I continue to be amazed at the enthusiasm she shows for this event in her life that will take her away from us, away from her orchestra, away from her cello, and into an unknown life of servitude to a husband—one Carlo Santi. The nuptial celebration is only three weeks away, and the future Signora Santi glows when she talks about her upcoming life on

Murano, the nearby island where the Santi family enjoys great success in the glass-blowing business. The only bit of the conversation that interests me in the least is the plan for our orchestra to play at the wedding Mass. It will be an impressive affair, she tells us, in line with her husband's social standing.

I wonder aloud about the dowry being paid by the *ospedale* to the Santi family. Where is that much money coming from? Cecilia is beautiful and intelligent, but we all know that a girl's family has to provide goods or money to the groom's family in order for a marriage to be arranged. I think there is some money kept back from each of our concerts to fund dowries, but still, enough to buy such a desirable match?

With a haughty bearing, Cecilia tips back her head and looks at me. "Ah, *Piccola Gatta*, now you are the curious cat, wondering about such things." Then she leans in over the table and continues in a low voice. "But I have also wondered about this, and I believe that one of the local nobles might have provided the means for my dowry."

"Why?" Monica asks innocently.

"Because he takes a special interest in my welfare," she answers with a lift of her eyebrows.

Understanding dawns on me. "You mean that this man was, or is, really your father?"

"I think so," she answers. "I have tried to think back over the receptions I've been invited to after concerts for the last couple of years, the people who spoke with me, and the one gentleman in particular who seemed to seek me out, ask after me, and care about my happiness." She shrugs her shoulders gracefully. "It would fit the puzzle that he is my father."

"Who is it?" Catherine whispers.

She shakes her head. "Because I'm not sure, I will not say."

I steal a look at Catherine, and she raises her eyebrows, sharing the mystery.

***

The next day, Don Vivaldi is late to our orchestra rehearsal. Our lives are ordered by the tolling of the bells, and we are all seated ready with our instruments at the appointed time. Usually punctual, Don Vivaldi comes in long after the bells directed us to be seated.

"I am late, girls," he says without apology, "because I had something important to finish." He drops a few pieces of paper on a side table before stepping in front of us.

We have a few rough spots to practice, but for the most part we sound good. I look at Cecilia sitting next to me and sigh. I don't expect her to play anymore after Easter. Monica sits at the side of the hall. She doesn't have to be here, but she likes to come to the rehearsals and watch us. As usual, she taps her little foot in perfect rhythm with the music. At the end of the session, Don Vivaldi catches my eye and motions me to the side of the room.

My heart somersaults in my chest! Is this the signal I've yearned for? Is it now my time to shine? My playing has been better than ever, and I know the *maestro* has noticed. I force myself to take a deep breath, and I walk slowly, not run clumsily, to where Don Vivaldi awaits.

*Concerto, my concerto,* my inner voice sings.

"I have something for you." He offers me the sheets of music he tossed on the table earlier. "Work on this with Monica. I don't want her just sitting in the orchestra. I want her to play, even if just a few simple notes."

Wordless, I look up at him and reach to take the music.

"It was very good of you," he says, "to think of her."

112

He leaves the room, and I stand motionless for a few moments. A hot flush rises from my neck to my face, and when I look at my hands, they are trembling. I replay the brief exchange at least ten times in my head, forcing myself to understand. Indeed, this is not about me. No, it is not my concerto.

I regain my composure because I am, after all, a disciplined musician, and I find Monica. "I have something very exciting to tell you," I say, the words stumbling over the lump in my throat.

That evening in the dining hall, as soon as Monica sees Signora Silvia, she runs to her and throws her arms around the matron's ample soft girth. "Don Vivaldi is letting me play on Holy Thursday!" Monica's joy twists her lips into a crooked smile.

"Oh, *mia cara*," exclaims Signora Silvia, throwing her arms around the girl. "This is such happy news. Oh, my, there is so much to think about—finding you a dress from the wardrobe, planning how to put your hair up, and whatever else...I cannot think right now."

Monica laughs, pulling a sound deeper from within than I've ever heard from her. "Playing my cello, Signora, playing my Felicità," she says. "That's what I'm thinking of. I am going to make my Felicità sing!" And then Monica breaks out of Signora's embrace and takes my hand. "And it's all because of Isabella," she says, squeezing my fingers, "*Maestra* Isabella, Don Vivaldi called her."

An impatient clearing of a gruff throat interrupts us. It is Signora Priora. "I need your assistance, Signora Silvia, if you could come with me, please."

Monica looks uncertainly between the two women and drops my hand.

Signora Silvia immediately obeys and turns to go, but before Signora Priora leaves us, she surveys me with an expression of cold calculation that I expect she uses when haggling with the butcher for the best value in meat. She turns her eye on Monica, and I take her hand and give it a squeeze of reassurance. Signora's gaze softens.

"Isabella dal Cello," she states in a monotone voice, "you are evidently doing a good job with your charge." She walks away with her imperious manner, and Monica looks up at me, now relaxing and half-smiling once more.

For the next couple of days, Monica and I focus our attention with even more determination on her playing as she prepares for the concert, but sometimes she worries me.

"Monica, you're breathing heavy again. Do you feel sick?"

"It's tight here," she says, pointing to her breastbone while she gulps. "But I want to play! Do I disappoint you?"

"Oh, no," I assure her. "You're doing a remarkable job. Don Vivaldi will be very pleased."

Of course, the deep disappointment I feel stems from the fact that I've not yet been chosen to play a solo in a concerto. But every time I have a lesson with Monica, the regret is softened by a proud delight in her accomplishments. She is good, after all, because I'm a good teacher. In that I am proud.

Don Vivaldi nods with satisfaction in our direction during Wednesday's orchestra rehearsal, and I look forward to Thursday's celebration of Christ's Last Supper. The next evening Signora Silvia clucks around Monica like a mother hen, adjusting her gown and smoothing her fine, wispy hair into a simple bun as we prepare for the Mass. I am confident that Monica is ready for her first public performance. She will play well. Cecilia takes one of Monica's hands in her own as we find our places in line.

"Monica, you look so pretty tonight, so pretty in your white gown," Cecilia says.

Monica shakes her head. "Oh, no, I'm not pretty...."

Cecilia interrupts. "But you are!" she insists. "You are beautiful. You are shining with radiance tonight."

I look at my charge with fresh eyes and see, as Cecilia does, how happiness has transformed Monica into a pretty girl. I hardly see her scars anymore.

With our instruments in hand, we file from the rehearsal hall down two flights to the choir loft in the church. We take our places, with Cecilia, Monica and me sitting close to the balcony railing. As I adjust the music sheets on the stand, I can't resist sneaking a peek into the crowded congregation below. I see him—that boy, Niccolò Morelli—looking back at me, and I can't restrain a smile. His lips curve into a slow grin.

However, when Don Vivaldi strides to the front of the orchestra for the prelude, my nerves sharpen, and I transfer all my attention to him. He bows elegantly to the assembly, and an expectant hush falls over the church. He stands erect, a magnificent sight in his red suit, *Il Prete Rosso*. I know that many of the people come not because they love music, but because they want to see the splendor of Don Antonio Vivaldi. All eyes below are now trained on the *maestro* and his orchestra. He raises his hands, but as he does, a shrill cackle disrupts the reverent silence. The disturbance catches us off guard, even our conductor.

With a lapse of self-discipline, I take my eyes off Vivaldi to see what's happening. Below, a richly dressed woman with an idiotically tall white wig is pointing up at us, telling her companions to look up. Only, she is not pointing up at all of us. She is pointing directly at my side—at Monica. When I understand, I turn to Monica, who now realizes that she's the cause of the commotion. She gasps rapidly a few times, and then a shadow of misery falls across her face and extinguishes the light in her eyes. She drops her head and shrinks into herself.

I look back in disbelief at the woman who is still making a spectacle of herself. With her heavily made-up face and blood-red lips, she whispers with a couple of her stupid friends as they all point at Monica's disfigurement. They think we are just a show. With anger welling up, I look at the Morellis. I am not sure why, but I want to see their reaction. Niccolò and his father both look at their hands in their laps, but Signora Morelli is looking down her hawk's nose at the disruptive group with an expression of righteous disgust.

After what seems a lifetime, but is only a couple of moments, Don Vivaldi turns from the orchestra to the congregation below. He stands tall, his shoulders back, and crosses his arms. The tension in the church is palpable as our daunting red-haired conductor stares unflinchingly at the rude woman. Within a few seconds, the man to the right of the woman nudges her, and she stops her cruel snickering. She directs her attention to Vivaldi and then demurely bows her head.

"Monica," I whisper, "Monica, look at me."

Monica remains rigid, her eyes downcast.

"She is stupid," I say, so that only Monica can hear. "Don't let her ruin this time for you. You can still play." Her bow is in her lap, her left hand loose on the neck of the cello.

When I feel the rest of the girls ready their instruments, I look at Vivaldi. He has turned back to the orchestra, and a tomblike hush envelopes the sanctuary. With his arms poised, he looks sideways at the cello section. Cecilia is ready. I am ready. I

116

can hear Monica's skirt rustling as she lifts her bow. I am fighting a tremble in my hands, but I play when it is time because I am a disciplined musician. So is Monica. When her passage comes, she forms her notes and moves her bow with technical precision, but that is all—just technical precision. Her cello does not sing today.

# Chapter Fifteen
## *The Mystery Screen*

I pause before the heavy wooden door. I detest coming to Signora Priora to beg a favor, but I detest even more the consequence of doing nothing.

I barely slept last night, frustration and anger about the horrid woman with blood-red lips pummeling my thoughts after I climbed into bed. Monica didn't sleep well either. I never heard the change in her breathing rhythm that would indicate she had succumbed to a deep slumber. All night long her breaths came weak and ragged while she lay next to me.

Last night, when the Holy Thursday service was over, Catherine and I flanked Monica on our way back to the rehearsal hall to put away our instruments. Monica moved as if she were in a trance, a veil of blankness clouding her eyes. She didn't look at me; she didn't look at Catherine. She didn't respond to any of our words. After climbing a few steps up the stairway, she paused, struggling to catch her breath. I took her cello, her Felicità. Catherine supported her arm to help her climb the rest of the way up. Every few steps she needed rest. As the other girls passed on their way up the stairs, they murmured words of kindness to Monica, but she didn't appear to hear them. She drew on a deep reserve of strength to complete her climb to the fourth floor, then she collapsed on a chair. Her face was pale, and her breathing came in ragged, shallow little gulps.

Offering no more resistance than a pile of rags, she let Catherine and me undress her, take her hair down, and tuck her into bed. Through the night my mind worked feverishly to plot a solution for this problem. I've been around the wealthy and privileged long enough to know that the vicious woman in the congregation last night is not the only one of her breed. Others will come behind that evil woman and make fun of Monica. Idea after idea tumbled through my head, and I struggled to justify a plan so that I can protect her.

But today I must concede this is not a problem I can solve. Regrettably, I must include Signora Priora if I want to prevent from happening again what happened last night. I grit my teeth as I stand here now and knock on her door.

"Come in," she calls in a curt voice.

I enter and stand before her desk. She has a journal open before her and a reading glass at its side. Her eyes squint as her finger runs up and down columns of numbers. I am determined this morning to follow all the rules of propriety, so I will not speak until she speaks to me first.

"Isabella dal Cello," she states flatly, looking up only briefly before returning her attention to her figures.

"Good morning, Signora." I clear my throat, feeling awkward in the company of the prioress. "I have come about Monica."

Signora nods. "I know about last night. I saw what happened." She looks at me now, and the wrinkles at the corners of her eyes relax.

I open my mouth, searching for just the right words, when Signora asks: "Do you think Monica should be taken out of the orchestra so this kind of thing cannot happen again?"

"Oh, no!" I am quick to protest. "Monica needs to play her cello with the orchestra. She must do that." What was it Signora said before? That nothing she does is about just one of us, but everything is for the whole?

120

I hastily think to add, "And the orchestra needs Monica. She is going to be very good. Even Don Vivaldi thinks so."

She lowers her quill and stares at me for several long moments in her unnerving way. "Then why are you here?" she asks at last.

"Because I think I have an idea, a plan that can work." I clasp my hands together. "A plan that can keep Monica in the orchestra but out of the public eye so she cannot be taunted again."

Signora Priora cocks her head in curiosity.

I send a prayer heavenward that she will consider my idea. "Signora, you said before that our *ospedale* has a fine reputation for protecting the virtue of the girls here."

She nods.

"So I have an idea, a plan that will help protect that reputation and help protect Monica from the cruelty of others."

*Clack...clack...clack.* Her teeth knock together. "What on earth are you talking about?" she snaps irritably.

"A screen."

"A screen?"

"Yes, Signora, a screen. What I envision is a kind of grille that goes across the front of the balcony. I don't think it would harm the sound of the music, but it would serve as a divider between the orchestra and the people below."

"Then the people couldn't see the orchestra."

"Exactly. Monica would be protected, but there would be another benefit as well. The virtue of the girls would be safeguarded because no man could have impure thoughts when he looked up."

Signora folds her hands, her index fingers to her lips. She tries to hide it, but I see a hint of a smile. "Isabella dal Cello," she says, "as I have always believed of you, you are a wily, scheming girl."

I know she will detect anything less than total honesty.

"Yes," I quietly agree, "perhaps I am. But in this case my motives are honorable."

"So you are saying that this grille, this screen, could keep Monica from being hurt again and at the same time enhance the reputation of the *Ospedale della Pietà?*"

"Yes. I could draw a picture for you to show you what I mean."

"I do not think I need your picture. But answer me this. You say you care about the reputation of the *ospedale*, which I believe affects the welfare of all the girls. But would you be standing before me right now if it were not for your concern for Monica?"

"No, Signora," I admit.

She unlinks her fingers and massages the furrows in her forehead. "I will think about it," she says at last.

I take a very deep breath. "Please, Signora Priora," I implore. "Please help do something for Monica. I would do anything—anything at all—to keep her from getting hurt like that again."

Once again I spy the merest suggestion of a smile on her face.

"It is certainly not something I can do on my own. Heavens, no! I will have to talk with Don Vivaldi, and if he agrees, *if* he agrees, then I will have to go to the board of governors."

"Thank you," I whisper.

"I make no promises," she says, shaking her head. "We have to be very careful not to jeopardize the generosity of the gifts from our patrons." She taps the figures on the page before her. "Last night was not good, Isabella dal Cello. The collection was less than expected, but I could feel the discomfort in the sanctuary. It made people very uneasy when Don Vivaldi had to stare at that awful woman. We need to avoid any such incident in the future."

I stand waiting.

"You are dismissed now," she says with a flourish of her hand.

As I turn the doorknob, I look back over my shoulder and ask: "How many girls did you feed yesterday, Signora Priora?"

"It was 744," comes her ready response. "No, wait; let me correct myself—it was 745."

As I leave her office, I notice Signora Silvia at the end of the hallway surrounded by several of the girls. It will be 746 today, I think, as I realize that Signora Silvia is holding a tiny bundle wrapped in filthy rags.

I approach the group as Signora Silvia asks, "What name shall be given to this tiny one?"

Gabriella speaks: "What about Veronica? We could name her for the saint who comforted Jesus on his way to the cross."

Signora Silvia nods approvingly. "Yes, Veronica is a good name, very good indeed. It would be very appropriate for a girl given to us on Good Friday. That will be her baptismal name."

I sigh with an inexplicable weariness. Where had my name come from? Why was I Isabella? The babies come so often that their arrival is not even remarkable, and I have never given much thought to where their names come from. With a parting look at the silent, black-headed infant, I leave to find Cecilia. We won't have a midday meal because we are fasting today. Instead, we will go to the church at noon, and I want to talk with Cecilia before then.

I find her in the garden, and I sit next to her. She listens with great concern when I relate to her the exchange I had with Signora Priora.

"Perhaps I can help," she says when I finish.

"How?"

She purses her lips as she considers a thought. "I will try to get a message to someone." She shrugs gracefully. "Maybe it won't help, but then again, maybe it will."

Monica doesn't go to church with us this afternoon. Signora Silvia takes her back to the infirmary because her breathing affliction is aggravated, and she hopes Signora Pellegrina can find a remedy. The chorus sings *a cappella* at the service remembering Christ's crucifixion, and the rest of us sit in the balcony. The sanctuary below is full, and I notice several of the school's governors in attendance.

At the end of the service, Cecilia steps up to the railing. Signor Coradini, the governor I met at the reception, notices Cecilia. He smiles, and motions to her. As the other girls leave the choir loft, Cecilia descends the steps from the balcony to the sanctuary and approaches the stately gentleman. I hang back in the recesses of the loft for a few moments to watch their exchange. Signor Coradini smiles warmly and extends both his hands to clasp hers. He then bows his head and listens carefully as she speaks. When Cecilia motions toward the balcony, he raises his head to follow the direction of her hand.

Later, Cecilia catches me in the rehearsal hall. "I saw you," she says. "I know you were spying on me, *Piccola Gatta*."

I shrug.

"No matter," she says. "We will wait and see if anything can be done."

Easter Sunday is a radiant day of celebration, and late that afternoon, Monica returns from the infirmary, looking much stronger.

"You smell sweet again," I tell her when she joins us at our Easter feast. "Did Signora Pellegrina treat you with honey and lavender oil today?" She nods. I tell her tomorrow we will resume lessons.

On Monday, she not only has a lesson with me, but sits in with the orchestra for rehearsal. When Don Vivaldi gives us our new music for the week, I see that once again he has written a simple passage for Monica.

On Thursday, when we go to the church for rehearsal, a twitter of excitement runs through the line of girls as they emerge from the *ospedale* into the choir loft. There, atop the balcony railing is a delicate grille of ornate wrought iron. The music can still flow through the apertures into the sanctuary, but the people below will have a difficult time seeing behind the screen. Don Vivaldi points out a gate, almost invisible in the screen, which can be opened if necessary.

Monica grips my wrist when she sees the new addition. "Thank you, Isabella."

That afternoon her cello sings. So does mine. Smiling, Don Vivaldi calls me aside after practice to tell me he hasn't forgotten about my lessons. I will start studying with him soon!

On Sunday afternoon, as is our tradition in Venice, the orchestra and chorus of the *Ospedale della Santa Maria* give a public concert. Hundreds of people stream into the sanctuary, both visitors and residents of the city. Even though we will be sheltered from view, we still take great care with our appearance. Earlier this day Signora Silvia called for Monica, and when Monica returned, she had feathery bangs that fell down over her forehead and curved around her eyes. Signora Silvia had pulled strands of hair from above Monica's ears so that gentle tendrils hung down her cheeks. Monica looks beautiful now with the harshness of her scars so artfully softened.

I find Cecilia in the rehearsal hall when I go to get Speranza. "Thank you," I tell her, "for whatever you said to help get the screen."

"You're welcome," she answers, and a single tear slides down her cheek. She brushes it with the back of her hand and looks away.

"Cecilia," I ask, "what's wrong?"

"My *Piccola Gatta*," she says with a wan smile, "today will be the only day I will ever play with that screen. Today is my last concert."

I look at her and smile. "Then today we will play the very best we can so we will always have this perfect memory."

And that is what we do. Today, not only the cellos, but the violins, the violas, the wind instruments, and all the others play with a most excellent flair. Don Vivaldi beams when the concert is over. I peek through an opening in the screen and look below as the vigorous appreciation fills the space. The crowd is looking up, straining their necks to see us as they shuffle their feet and blow their noses. The Morelli family sits below, and Niccolò is anxiously searching the divider. I have the oddly warm feeling that he is seeking me.

On buoyant feet I return to our building to put away Speranza. Cecilia stands in the rehearsal hall with her cello, as though caressing it, savoring these last few moments.

126

"You played really well today," I say. "Probably the best you ever have. Are you sure you want to proceed down the path to marriage?" I ask, tilting my head.

She sighs with a serenity that is uniquely her own. "Yes. I have known great happiness here, but I want more, Isabella. I know that I am making the right choice for me."

A brusque voice interrupts us, and I turn with a sense of dread to see Signora Priora approaching.

"Isabella dal Cello," she calls crisply, "what did you think of the performance today?"

"I thought it went very well," I confidently answer. "The new screen is perfect."

"Evidently you are not the only one who thinks so," she says, holding up a bulging pouch. "The coins from today's collection are in here. I have not had a chance to count yet, but I think this is one of our most lucrative concerts yet."

"The governors should be well pleased," says Cecilia.

"Yes," answers Signora Priora, "because the money is always necessary. Today we are lucky to find that Venice loves the mystery of what she cannot see more than the certainty of what she can."

# Chapter Sixteen
## *The Wedding*

Cecilia's wedding is only a day away, and we are giddy with anticipation! The plans grow more elaborate every day as we receive new details about what we will play, what we will wear, and how we will walk into the church. I ponder this as it relates to Monica, but I hope that the wedding guests will be better behaved than the tourists who visit Venice on holiday. The *maestro* is writing a simple part for Monica so that she can play with the orchestra at the wedding, and Monica will not be hidden from the congregation as we process into the sanctuary. Don Vivaldi is laboring feverishly to complete the music for the wedding Mass, and I think he has written the grandest parts for the cellos, probably to honor Cecilia's former role as principal.

After lunch Signora Priora calls us outside for practice. We all go through the courtyard onto the *calle* that runs along the side of the *ospedale* to rehearse the processional. There are about sixty musicians, and of course, several of the matrons accompany us. Signora Pellegrina is going to play her violin with us. She says that she cannot miss Cecilia's nuptial celebration, so nobody is allowed to get sick and require her ministrations.

Signora Priora lines us all up, straight and orderly, in her quest for perfection. Monica is behind me; Catherine is in front of me. Over and over, our prioress makes us take our places and fusses with our arrangement. She leads us up the lane to the *fondamenta* fronting the Grand Canal. As I step from the shadows of the narrow street into the open space in front of the church with the sun-drenched vista of the *Canale di San Marco,* the large body of water in front of our *ospedale,* my heart soars to see the world beyond our walls.

Tourists and residents alike stop along the sidewalk to watch. To the onlookers, we must present quite a spectacle— Don Vivaldi's orphan musicians all dressed alike in our dowdy dull red dresses, some of us holding our instruments, some of us holding unlit candles. With Monica's new hairstyle, her face is not as conspicuous; yet, she keeps her head down when she is close to the outsiders. Because she is being so careful to hide her face, she is not one of the first girls to call attention to the graceful ship with English markings that is sailing up the lagoon.

"Girls," Signora Priora calls with a sharp clap of her hands, "pay attention to me." But we do not heed her call, as one by one all of us turn to watch the beautiful sloop gliding past on its way to the quay close to the *Piazza* San Marco. One of the sailors in the rigging waves. Catherine is the first to wave back, and then before we can be stopped, a whole host of girls and a multitude of sailors are smiling at each other across the water and waving greetings.

"Stop that. Now!" Signora Priora hisses. "It is not proper. This is not how the young ladies from the *Ospedale Santa Maria della Pietà* should behave!"

Behind me, Monica keeps her head down, but she giggles at Signora's futile effort. There in the embrace of the warm spring sunshine, we are a small congenial crowd enjoying the arrival of yet another ship to Venice. When it is past us, we resume our practice, now tedious with repetition, and most of the onlookers wander away.

Over and over we practice lining up, with one vocalist next to each instrumentalist. We will have our hands occupied with our cellos, violins, and other instruments, but the singers will each carry two lit votive candles during the actual ceremony when we process from the courtyard to make a grand entrance into the church. Cecilia will be the final member of the processional line, and she watches the rest of us with pride and enthusiasm. At last, Signora Priora signals that we are done. As our prioress dismisses us, messengers bearing a carefully wrapped packet approach our group from the side of the *ospedale* where the gondola landing is situated, the side opposite the church.

"*Buongiorno,*" calls one. "We are looking for Signorina Cecilia, the bride-to-be, I believe." He doffs his hat and bows deeply from his waist in a grand theatrical gesture. "We bear a gift from the island of Burano."

Signora Priora steps forward briskly. "I can take it," she declares, holding out her arms.

"Not necessary," calls a competing voice as Cecilia makes her way to the front of the throng of girls. "I am the one you are looking for."

Confused, the messenger looks from the stern-faced matron to the equally resolute young woman approaching him.

"I will take it," says Cecilia firmly, extending her hand to him. He looks at Signora Priora, who scowls and shrugs, and then he relinquishes the package to its rightful recipient.

"What is it?" cries Catherine, straining her neck in excited anticipation.

Signora sharply claps her hands twice. "Cecilia can take it inside to open it. Young women from the *Ospedale della Pietà* do not stand outside in public to open packages."

131

Cecilia stands rooted in place and looks down at the packet cradled carefully in her hands. "Begging your pardon, Signora Priora, but I think that I will open my gift out here so that all my friends might share in my excitement."

A quiet, shocked gasp filters through us, and Signora draws herself up to her full height and narrows her eyes. "As you wish."

I, probably more than anybody, appreciate and admire Cecilia's gesture of rebellion. I cheer happily when she takes a note from the wrapping paper. She holds it up with a flourish and reads: "To Cecilia, a dear young woman of the *Ospedale della Pietà*--We wish you a lifetime of joy as you fulfill your duty to God and family." We all nod in appreciation as she lowers the sheet of stationery and adds, "It is signed *Signor Coradini and Family*."

"So, go on now," urges Catherine, "a present from one of our governors—open it so we can all see what it is."

Signora Priora stands with her arms folded across her chest, her lips bunched in clear disapproval, but she remains silent.

"Come here, Monica," instructs Cecilia. "You hold the package while I untie the strings." Monica rushes forward to help.

Very deliberately, very adroitly, Cecilia unties each of the three strings that bind the paper around the treasure. When the strings are undone and hanging loose, she pauses before peeling back the covering. Monica, shaping her mouth into her smile, looks up at Cecilia with expectancy. Cecilia raises her eyebrows and carefully reaches into the folds of paper to withdraw the treasure. Ever so deliberately she takes out and then unfolds a frothy confection of dove-white lace. She lets it drape over one arm.

A murmur of appreciation runs through the girls as she holds the lace veil higher. Monica secures the bottom of it so that it does not touch the ground. A tremor of awe snakes down my spine. I am an orphan and have nothing. But I am an orphan who has witnessed the trappings of the rich and privileged, and I am aware of quality workmanship. This veil from Burano is a work of art, with its fine and intricate pattern that was hand-worked by several lace makers unerring in their attention to detail.

"It is beautiful," Cecilia whispers in awe, as her eyes travel over the generous length of lace. "It is beautiful," she repeats.

It is indeed, I think, a very kind gift from Signor Coradini.

"Hold it over your head," suggests Catherine, and several others echo her.

Cecilia very cautiously finds the top end of the veil and artfully places it over her auburn hair while Monica holds on to the train of the veil.

Gabriella starts clapping and then the others join in, even Signora Pellegrina. Signora Priora huffily instructs the group to return to the courtyard and lets Cecilia lead the way. The girls fall into line behind her, but I hang back.

I love being outside, especially outside the walls of our compound. I love seeing the people on the walkways, the boats on the water, and the gulls in the sky. I look across the calm waters of the lagoon at the *campanile* of San Giorgio Maggiore, the special place where I was able to see the whole world. I close my eyes, momentarily savoring that wonderful memory, and when I open them again, I see that there are only two other girls waiting to head toward the courtyard, and I move in their direction.

133

Signora Priora steps forward to shoo us along, but she pauses as something behind me catches her attention. I look over my shoulder in the direction of the *Piazza* San Marco and see a young boy jogging toward us. He might be a ship's boy.

"*Scusi!*" he cries as he comes closer, "a letter, a message." He waves an envelope in the air.

Signora puts up her right hand to shield her eyes from the slanting sun, and her face adopts an air of wariness as she realizes he is coming toward us. She eyes me abruptly and orders, "Go on now, Isabella dal Cello. This has nothing to do with you."

I move toward the shadowed *calle* that leads to our courtyard, but seized with curiosity, I pause.

The boy is surely younger than I. He wears a worn shirt and tattered dungarees, and he pads barefoot across the cobblestones. He stops a few feet from the imposing figure of Signora Priora and asks in a foreign accent, "*Ospedale della Pietà?*"

Signora nods slowly. "*Sì,*" she answers.

"A letter for you," he says, "*un messaggio.*"

"*Grazie,*" she replies, reaching into the deep well of the pocket hidden in the folds of her grey dress and withdrawing a small coin for him.

"Thank you," he grins. "*Grazie.*" He hands her an envelope and turns back toward the *Piazza*. I look now and see in the distance that the English ship that arrived earlier is now moored right at the entrance to the *Piazza San Marco*, and sailors mill busily on the dock, unloading countless boxes of freight.

"Isabella dal Cello!"

I hear the sharp reprimand in Signora Priora's voice as she calls me down. "I told you this has nothing to do with you. Now go on and attend to your duties."

That evening after supper we rehearse for one last time the music for Cecilia's wedding. The composition that Don Vivaldi has labored over this week is, I believe, one of the most beautiful that the *maestro* has ever created, and I find it very sad that Cecilia will not be playing with us. I am so proud of Monica, though, because she is playing her part with a grace and joy that make her cello sing.

After practice is over, Signora Priora comes into the hall and approaches Don Vivaldi. I am organizing my sheets of music when I hear her tell him that she is concerned about a very curious letter that she has received. With a worried expression on her face, she asks him to stop by her office and discuss the matter with her later. This is a curious matter, yes, but it is not nearly as exciting as the prospect of the wedding extravaganza. Visions of girls in white dresses playing cellos fill my dreams during the night.

I awaken before the bells call me, and I can't help waking Monica. She is already awake, however, her weak puffs of breath marking an irregular rhythm.

"I thought about the wedding all night," she rasps, "and how I will get to play with the orchestra."

"There has never been another wedding like Cecilia's," I say. "I could hardly sleep for the excitement."

Cecilia is kept apart from us during the day, and as the sun starts to sink, we all go to the wardrobe area to dress. I help Catherine twist her blonde hair into a chignon, and she braids

135

my hair and then pins it up. Signora Silvia comes to help Monica with her hair, once again combing her bangs around her face and pulling a couple of soft tendrils from over her ears to fall across the scars of her cheeks. For this special occasion, as for our public concerts, we all don our white dresses.

"Monica, are you feeling okay?" questions Signora Silvia as she puts her hands on Monica's shoulders and looks her in the face. Monica is once again breathing with shallow, raspy breaths, and her complexion is tinged gray.

"I am fine," she says weakly. "I want to play."

"Don't be nervous, *mia cara*," says Signora Silvia, taking Monica's face in her plump hands. "I heard you at rehearsal, and you sounded wonderful."

We gathered our instruments, and Monica holds hers with difficulty.

"I'll trade you," I say, holding out my bow to her and taking her cello. It's no trouble for me to carry two cellos.

The soft, gray shadows of dusk fall over Venice, and Signora Silvia leads us from the courtyard of the *ospedale* out onto the *calle* where she and a couple of the other matrons line us up in the precise manner we had practiced. Catherine is in front of me and Monica is directly behind. Signora Pellegrina is behind Monica, and as old as she is, she stands erect holding her violin. Next to each of us is a vocalist holding two candles. Matrons pass down the line of girls, lighting the wicks and setting the shadowed lane atwinkle. Then we march up the path to the *fondamenta* where we wait at the edge of the large canal. Torches at the water's edge are lit.

The velvet haze of evening deepens, and Don Antonio Vivaldi, violin in hand, approaches us from the church. He takes up position at the water's edge and starts playing. Don Vivaldi is, and forever in my mind, will be, a genius of the violin. He plays a beautiful, soul-wrenching melody, one I do not remember hearing before.

I turn to Monica, and she watches the *maestro* with rapt admiration. "He is improvising," I whisper. Then a murmur draws my attention back to Signora Silvia. She puts her hand to her chest in a gesture of amazement, and my gaze follows hers. Cecilia steps from the darker lane into the light cast by the glowing torches. She stands radiantly magnificent, dressed in her white wedding finery. I know that her gown is simply one of the nicer concert dresses, but the Burano lace veil framing her face, cascading down and over her shoulders, gives her the regal look of an ancient, mythical goddess—Venus at her most beautiful. Even in the growing dark, I can tell that Cecilia beams a joyous, broad smile.

One of the little girls, maybe five- or six-years-old, steps out from behind Cecilia carrying a basket of pomegranate petals, and makes her way to the front of the line, daintily scattering the petals as she skips along.

I turn and whisper to Monica, "Cecilia is the most beautiful thing I have ever seen." Monica mutely grips her bow a little tighter and nods. She tries to form a little smile. "Are you okay?" I ask. She nods, but doesn't speak.

A black gondola, drawn by the magnet of Vivaldi's violin, glides close to the edge of the lagoon. Several richly garbed people sit inside, and one exclaims, "They look like angels!"

Don Vivaldi ends his serenade and makes his way back to the church. Signora Silvia and the other women exchange wordless signals among themselves and start the procession moving. The instrumentalists walk on the building side of the sidewalk, while the singers walk next to the water's edge. The reflection of the many tiny votive candles twinkles on the lagoon like a field of stars. Goose bumps prickle up my arms as I walk, the pride swelling inside me because I am part of this enchanted, magical moment.

We march with precision along the walkway, into the grand doors of the church, up the middle aisle, and then climb the sanctuary's interior staircase up to the choir loft. I don't turn to look at Monica behind me, but I guess that she's keeping her head bowed as we pass through the crowd. I still carry both cellos, and even though she carries only two bows, I hear her breath, excessively labored.

After we settle into our places, Don Vivaldi steps to the rostrum, his shoulders tall and erect. Tonight he is the vision of *Il Prete Rosso*, the red priest, in his scarlet suit. For the formality of this occasion, he has covered his long locks with his powdered white wig. He raises his hands, and bliss suffuses me as we begin to play the triumphant processional music. Tonight I regret the screen because it impedes my view of the wedding below, but when I hear a stunned gasp of astonishment ripple through the congregation, I know that our Cecilia has appeared in the sanctuary. Our Cecilia, an abandoned girl of unknown origins, is marching up the aisle to a marriage into one of Venice's best and most respected families. Even as I play, I pray that the path before her satin-slippered feet will lead her to a lifetime of abundant joy.

The nuptial Mass, rich with ritual and tradition, begins with a blessing. After several readings, the vows are dutifully exchanged, and even though I cannot see my dear friend's face, I can tell by the firm tone of her responses that she marries with no regrets. I think I hear in her new husband's voice a measure of respect and devotion.

Several times during the ceremony, I reach over and squeeze Monica's hand, hoping to impart some strength and encouragement. As the ceremony drags on, though, Monica's energy fades, and her grasp on her cello is weak. When the newly wedded couple turns to march down the aisle, I take up my bow for the recessional hymn. Startled, I hear a clatter next to me, and I avert my eyes from Don Vivaldi to see that Monica's bow has fallen to the floor. Both of her hands are gripped in tight fists around the neck of her Felicità. She stares vacantly ahead, her face ashen, and her small chest heaves with sharp, staccato breaths that seize her body.

*What do I do?* My mind cries! From the corner of my eye, I see Signora Pellegrina lay down her violin and step to Monica. She kneels next to her, supporting her body and keeping her from falling from her chair.

My heart slams in my chest, but I drag my eyes back to Don Vivaldi with all the resolve of a trained musician. We must complete the final piece. Cecilia's wedding cannot be ruined! Simply going through the motions, I form chords on the cello's strings, run the bow over the strings, and manage to play every note that I'm supposed to play. All the while a black specter of fear wells within me. At last, when Vivaldi signals the final note, I quickly lay down Speranza and grab Monica's cello. I pry her fingers off the instrument and gently lay it on the floor next to mine. Then I reach for Monica, and Signora Pellegrina lets her slump unconsciously against me. Terrified, my heart kicking, I keep my arm around her shoulders until Signora Silvia materializes on the other side of her.

"Shhh," whispers Signora Silvia to Signora Pellegrina and me, cocking her head toward the sanctuary down below where the wedding congregation is making its way outside. She kneels and gently gathers Monica's limp form against her soft, plump chest. Dread courses through my body, and my legs grow weak. I'm not sure I can stand right now. I look around and see that Signora Priora is ever so quietly ushering the musicians, not down the staircase we had come up earlier, but out the door that leads directly from the choir loft into the second floor of our *ospedale*.

Signora Silvia softly croons into Monica's ear, while Signora Pellegrina carefully feels the underside of Monica's wrist with her fingers. Signora Silvia nods to Don Vivaldi as he approaches us. "We will carry her out when all the others are gone," she says. "Together we should have no problem getting her to the infirmary."

"I can help too," I hear my voice say. "I want to help."

Don Vivaldi squeezes my shoulder. "You help by taking your cello and hers and see that they are put away. Then you can come check on your friend."

When the last girl exits the choir loft, Signora Priora joins us, brushing me aside to get close to Monica.

"You may leave now, Isabella."

"Please, Signora," I implore, "let me follow Monica."

"So be it," she says in her usual terseness, and turns to help lift Monica. The three of them hoist her limp form and in careful synchronization, carry her back to the *ospedale*. Signora Pellegrina follows, her violin forgotten on the floor, and I follow last.

"Please, God. Please, God. Please, God." I try to frame a meaningful prayer but no other words will come.

"Please, God."

# Chapter Seventeen
## *Finding Grace*

Whispers of plague scurry through the halls of the *ospedale*. Even the little girls who don't know what the term means become frightened by the very word. When the fearful rumor reaches Signora Silvia's ears, she is quick and unwavering in tamping it down.

"By all the holy saints!" she swears when she emerges from the infirmary and hears the gossip. "Monica does not have the plague. There is no threat of plague here."

Several pairs of wary eyes watch her skeptically. "Listen to me," she says with a note of harsh frustration. "I know the plague. I have seen the plague, and what Monica suffers from is not the plague."

Catherine shifts her feet uneasily and takes a deep breath before speaking hesitantly. "How can you be sure, Signora Silvia?"

Signora Silvia is fatigued from spending long hours by Monica's side, and her patience snaps. "Catherine, I know. I have seen the plague, and this is not the plague. Instead of questioning me, spend your time saying some extra prayers for your young friend. And then reassure your friends and classmates not to be scared. This is just a silly rumor spread by silly girls who have nothing better to do than repeat gossip!" She shakes her head in irritation and walks away.

Catherine looks as though Signora Silvia slapped her. We have never heard her use such a sharp tone with anybody. I am almost too tired to wonder at Signora Silvia's behavior. In the two nights and two days since Monica's collapse, I haven't been allowed to do anything to help, so my worry for Monica festers inside me with increasing pressure. Every time I ask after her, the answer is the same: "No change." Signora Pellegrina has not left the infirmary, but has stayed constantly by Monica's side.

So I go to the chapel and pray several times a day and make all sorts of bargains with God. I look at our beautiful statue of Mary holding Jesus, cradling him so tenderly, and try to see some message about Monica. Mostly though, I feel helpless, and the helplessness fills me with an unnerving exhaustion. After supper, Catherine and I go out to the garden and move to the stone bench in the far corner.

The balmy night is swathed in moonless darkness, so we feel, rather than see, that someone is already on our bench as we approach.

"Hello, my girls," comes the tired, but welcoming voice. "I am trying to get a little rest before I go back in, but I would love for you to join me." Signora Silvia pats the stone seat next to her, but Catherine takes a step backwards.

"Oh, Catherine," Signora Silvia says, "I am sorry for the way I snapped at you. I am not myself right now. Please come and sit down."

Catherine glances at me, and then sits on one side of Signora Silvia. I find a place on the other. The woman sighs heavily. "I would like to tell you a little story," she says. "It should answer your question about how I can be sure that Monica does not have the plague."

"A story?" I ask, intrigued. "Who is the story about?"

"Someone who does not exist anymore," she answers tiredly, putting an arm around each of us. "This is not a fairy tale, but I will begin with 'Once upon a time'." Signora gazes heavenward and ponders the stars for a few moments before continuing. Catherine and I wait anxiously.

Then, she begins, "Once upon a time, far from Venice, there lived a young woman who thought she had found paradise on earth. She married a young man chosen for her by her parents. The young man was good and kind, even funny. Not too far into this marriage the young husband and wife became good friends. They laughed a lot. And she grew to love him very much."

I smile. "So this is a love story then?"

"Ah, wait until the end before you say," says Signora Silvia, and she continues. "So the young husband and wife were filled with joy when they had a baby girl the first spring following their marriage. The next spring they had another baby girl, and the next spring they had yet a third! The young man teased his bride about her failure to produce a son, but he doted on his girls.

"Their life was not easy, but it was pleasant. They worked with his family who had a hostel for pilgrims traveling on their way to and from Rome. Hundreds of travelers stopped in at their place for a night's rest and a hot meal. The travelers shared news from all over the continent and beyond, and occasionally there would be tense whispers of the black threat."

She sighs heavily. "And then it all came to an end. Their idyllic life loving each other and taking care of their baby girls came to an end. One group of travelers brought with them that which is feared above all—the Black Death—the plague. The young husband was the first to fall ill and die. His wife stayed by his side and did all she could for him, but without success. Other family members fell sick also, including the baby, and still the young woman did all she could to help the ill. In too short a

143

time, she had to tell her littlest one goodbye, and then the second…and then the third."

Signora Silvia's chest heaves with a silent sob, but I sit unmoving. She resumes her tale: "This woman knew the plague—knew its symptoms and signs more than any living person ought to know it. With death all around her, she waited for her turn, anxious to join her husband and babies. But in the cruelest twist of all, she lived."

Catherine shifts on the other side of Signora Silvia and whispers gently, "That was you, wasn't it?"

"That woman was hardly me. That woman existed in a fog for days, even weeks. She did not want to eat, but could not resist her hunger. She wanted to lie down and die, but the pull of life was too strong. She would have gone crazy, but she was rescued by a group of nuns on their way back to Venice from the Vatican. They took her to their convent, many days journey away, cleaned her up, and made her rest. They were determined to save her. She slept for days and days, and when she woke up, really woke up, the nuns took her to the *Ospedale della Pietà* where they had secured a position for her. She was to take care of babies and children. It was the only thread of life that she had to hold onto. Her heart was still broken, and she did not understand why God had spared her, but she had faith there was a reason for it."

This time I interrupt her. "That was you, wasn't it?"

She nods. "Yes, that was me. And you girls, all of you girls here at the *Pietà*, are the reason God saved me. I knew when I was brought here why God had spared me. I lost my daughters; you lost your mothers. This is my calling."

"So you have seen the plague close up," says Catherine wonderingly, "but you survived it. That's how you know that Monica doesn't have the plague."

"What our little Monica has is an affliction of weak breathing. Her little body can hardly take in enough air. When one of you takes a deep breath, you can feel it all the way down here." Signora Silvia pats the bottom of her stomach. "You are able to draw air all the way down to the pit of your gut. But our little Monica—when she tries to take a breath, she cannot get it past here." Signora pats her upper chest. "And when I lay my ear against her, I hear a noise like a muffled rattle." Signora shakes her head. "Signora Pellegrina is trying one poultice after another, but there is no relief for Monica yet."

"But she will get well, yes?" I hasten to say. "She's been sick before, but she got better."

Signora Silvia starts to rise, and she turns sympathetic eyes on me. "God's will be done," she says simply.

"But can she go to the country to breathe in the fresh air? I know that some of the other girls have been taken to the country to recover when they were sick."

"That is true," Signora says, "and Signora Pellegrina has considered that, but she thinks that moving Monica would do her more harm than good. So she will stay here with us."

I stand up and nervously grab Signora's arm. "But she will get well!"

Signora turns and takes my face gently in her hands and kisses my forehead. "I cannot give you any promise, Isabella. But I will go back in now and do all that I can for her."

Wordlessly, Catherine and I watch Signora disappear into the darkness, and then we reach for each other's hands.

"Poor Signora Silvia," mutters Catherine as she squeezes my hand.

"Poor Monica," I whisper as I return the gesture.

Two more days pass with no improvement on Monica's part. More and more often, I find myself drawn to the rehearsal hall, and I lose myself for hours playing my cello. Life in the *ospedale* does not stop because one girl is sick; routine in the *ospedale* cannot stop for anybody. Don Vivaldi writes a new piece for Sunday's performance, and the orchestra rehearses on schedule. But I come early before practice, and I stay late, savoring the solid presence of my beloved Speranza. When I play, I feel as though I'm playing for Monica. My Speranza sings with a beautiful voice.

On Thursday afternoon, I once again seek refuge in the corner of the garden, in the shade of the pomegranate tree. For five days now, Monica has been sick, and still I am not allowed to see her. I worry about her. I miss her. I sit alone and savor my solitude, listening to the chirps of birds and the distant sounds of footsteps on the *calle* beyond our walls. The bells call me to supper, but I ignore them. Now I can't tolerate the crowd in the dining hall. As the sun sinks behind the buildings and shadows engulf my little corner, someone approaches.

"Isabella," I hear the soft call, "Isabella, it is I."

"I'm here, Signora Silvia."

Signora Silvia ambles toward me with a slow, worn-out gait. As she gets close, I stand, and she engulfs me with a powerful embrace, the scent of lavender clinging to her. She wraps her arms around me and pulls me to her with firm pressure. She lays her cheek against mine. I start in panic when I feel that her cheek is moist.

"What's wrong?" I ask huskily. "Has Monica...?" I can't complete my terrible question.

She releases her hold and pulls me down to sit beside her on the stone bench. She shakes her head. "No," she answers. "But I need you to do something, *mia cara*."

"What?"

"I want to take you to see Monica. She has been asking for you this afternoon."

A sense of relief floods over me. "I would love to go see Monica," I exclaim. "I have missed her so much!"

"She has been missing you, too." Then Signora Silvia puts her arm around my shoulder and squeezes tenderly. "But I need to warn you, Isabella, that she is very, very sick."

"Maybe I can make her feel better," I say hopefully.

Signora Silvia nods. "Yes, I think you will make her feel better, but I do not think she will get well."

Her words make no sense. "What do you mean?" I ask haltingly.

"What I mean is very, very difficult to say. I want you to go and see Monica and tell her goodbye. Tell her it is okay for her to go."

The words sink in, and I recoil from Signora and jump up. "No!" I take a deep, painful breath and hug my arms tightly against myself. "No!" I repeat vehemently. A terrible black anxiety engulfs me. "No!" I cry again. "Monica cannot leave me too!"

Several silent moments pass. In the gathering gloom, I watch Signora Silvia clasp her hands together. "No," I assert even more defiantly. "I won't go see her to say goodbye!"

Signora entreats me with palms extended. "Please, Isabella," she implores, "come back and sit down with me."

I don't want to. I want to leave, perhaps sneak out the gate and run into the alleyways of Venice, but I surrender at last to her request and take my place once again on the bench. Signora reaches for my hands and holds them firmly.

"This is not about what you want," she says. "This is about what is best for Monica. Our little Monica is struggling for every breath she takes, each one more difficult than the one before. But she is fighting hard, and one of the main reasons is that she does not want you to feel as though she deserted you."

"But, Signora, I don't want her to leave. I cannot let her leave me too."

"I understand how difficult this is. It is painful for me too. But as I said, this is about your doing what is best for Monica — not thinking about what you want."

"It seems cruel to tell her goodbye, and I will not be cruel to her."

Signora Silvia shakes her head sadly. "No, *mia cara*, it is a kindness, because if you tell her goodbye, that it is okay for her to go, her passing will be more peaceful."

My voice ekes out a plea hardly more than a whisper. "Maybe she isn't going to die this time."

"I wish with all my heart and soul that Monica would get better, but all my experience tells me otherwise. Signora Pellegrina feels the same way. Sometimes we find grace in accepting the inevitable. My dear Isabella, I more than anybody know how hard this is."

Signora Silvia leaves me alone then and asks me to think about her request. She says that she cannot and will not force me to come see Monica. In painful solitude, I think about my young friend. I resented her presence when she first came, but now she is like a little sister to me. I have to act like a big sister now.

148

I do not yet feel the grace, but I do feel the responsibility that is mine. Signora Priora made her my responsibility. I will face the inevitable. I walk through the halls of the *ospedale* toward the infirmary, its pull an irresistible magnet. I have to brace myself with a deep breath when I arrive. The grace is not yet upon me.

The soft shadows of flickering candles dance on the wall behind Monica's bed. When I come in, Signora Silvia rises from Monica's side and sets down a pewter mug. "Monica was just enjoying some ginger and honey tea," she says. "Now I will leave you girls together." Signora hugs me, and whispers that she will be nearby. She pulls the curtains around Monica's bed before she pads away. The sweet scent of lavender haunts the air, and I can't help inhaling deeply.

I take the seat vacated by Signora Silvia, cocooned inside the drawn curtains, and I reach for Monica's hand. It is weak in my own, and I squeeze it very gently. "You missed practice again," I say in mock seriousness.

In the dimness, I see her open her eyes, and she tries to smile at me. She exerts great effort to speak, her breath coming in feeble little puffs. "I don't think ..." and she halts, unable to go on. I remain silent and wait. After a few moments, she continues, "...I can play anymore." Every syllable is a hard-fought labor.

So this is it, the moment when I must seize grace, even if it isn't obvious to me. I face the most important decision of my life when I try to think how I should respond. "It's okay if you don't play anymore," I say at last. "You know, you've been a most excellent musician, and the best kind of student. You have made me so happy because you came here. I want you to know how happy you have made all of us."

A couple of rapid breaths weaken her, and her grey eyes lock on my green eyes. She feebly squeezes my hand. "You…didn't…want me."

I nod as I swallow a lump. "Only at first, but then everything changed. I was relieved—so relieved—that first night when I saw that you had not been branded with the 'P'! I didn't want you to be hurt. I never wanted you to be hurt." I stroke her fingers and continue, "But when you gave your cello a name, when you said she was your Felicità, I knew you were the sister of my heart."

"Isabella…" she rasps, my name barely a whisper. "My sister."

"I'm here."

"You won't…," she pauses to breathe, "be mad…at me?"

I struggle to control my voice. "Of course I won't be mad at you, I promise. I understand that you can't play anymore." Signora Silvia's wisdom urges me on. "And Monica, it's okay for you to leave now. I understand, I truly do, and I wish you God's blessings."

I stroke her puckered forehead, pushing back a wisp of stray hair. The basin of lavender oil and water is at the side of her bed, along with a soft linen cloth. I wet the cloth and tenderly wipe Monica's forehead, her cheeks, and her throat. "And I give you my blessing," I add.

It is as though Monica relaxes into the bedding. "Thank you," she utters. She tries to lean up, her efforts to speak becoming harder. "Isa…bella…my sis…ter."

The vise grip on my heart tightens. "You are my sister too, and I love you," I whisper.

She tries to squeeze my hand. "Sis…ter."

The image of our statue of the *Pietà* comes to mind. "You can go to sleep now," I say, "and I'll stay here with you, right here by your side."

Monica barely nods her head and relaxes into the bed. I put down the cloth and pull the chair as close to the bed as I can. She closes her eyes. I contort myself so that I lift Monica's upper body and cradle her head against my shoulder. I drop my head against hers and hum softly. The melody that comes to mind is the triumphant recessional of Cecilia's wedding, her passage to her new life.

The feather-soft breaths that escape Monica's lips come further and further apart, but she doesn't struggle. I pray that the path before Monica will be one of joy and reward, and I feel the calm assurance that it will.

After some time, she does not inhale again. Her chest is absolutely still. I don't cry—not now. I enfold her even more closely against my body and kiss the top of her head and tell her farewell one last time. And now grace finds me, because it feels indescribably peaceful to have this gift of telling her goodbye. It was a gift I didn't have with my mother.

When Signora Silvia comes back into the room, I carefully lower Monica and rise and embrace the woman who is my friend. "Thank you," I whisper hoarsely.

I leave the infirmary and climb the stairs to the rehearsal hall. Dawn breaks, and the first rays of morning sun find me sitting with Felicità, Monica's cello. I wipe the smooth wood over and over again with the red silk cloth I had given Monica at one of our lessons. Catherine comes looking for me, and I tell her what happened.

"She was our little sister," I say.

"We are all sisters," Catherine answers. I reach out to Catherine and bury my head against her shoulder, and then we cry. The bells toll, but we ignore them, choosing to remain here with Monica's cello. Signora Priora peeks in on us, but doesn't disturb us. A torrent of tears flows from the two of us for hours, but we are quiet with red-rimmed eyes when Don Vivaldi comes into the hall about mid-morning.

"I am so sorry, girls," he says simply. "I am so very sorry." He pauses uncomfortably. "I want to do the right thing today."

I understand what he's really asking. "I think Monica would want us to go ahead and practice today," I answer.

He nods appreciatively. "The two of you do not have to rehearse. I understand your grief."

"I have to play!" I assert. "I have to play for both myself and Monica."

"I want to play too," agrees Catherine.

Our rehearsal that afternoon is bittersweet, our sadness tempered by our joy in offering up the music to Monica's memory. That night, with tears on her cheeks, Catherine comes and climbs into the bed with me and Gabriella. Monica's funeral Mass is said the next morning in our church of *Santa Maria della Pietà*. The liturgy celebrating Monica's new life comes only six days after the ritual celebrating Cecilia's new marriage. As the recessional hymn is sung, we follow her simple casket as it is borne out of the sanctuary to the front sidewalk.

A black gondola is moored at the landing right in front of the church. I take deep gulps of air as Monica's casket is carefully stowed aboard the craft. I can't help looking past the gondola across the large canal to the *campanile* of San Giorgio, the bell tower where Monica gave such effort to climb so that she

152

could see the whole world. I can't even imagine what she sees now.

Somebody grasps my elbow. "I would like you to come with me," says Signora Priora. "Monica was your responsibility, so I think it is right that you come with us to the cemetery."

For only the second time in my life, I board a gondola, but this time the gondolier takes us up the canal toward the cemetery. I lay my hand on the casket where Monica's body rests. I am grateful to make this final journey beside her. My hand remains on the casket for the entire journey.

# Chapter Eighteen
## *Dreams and Despair*

"Monica," I whisper, "you should be here to take your lesson with me." In the weeks since her death, I think of her constantly. I bite the inside of my lip as I run my fingers over the neck of Monica's cello, Felicità.

In the deepest part of my heart, I yearn to be angry at her. I want to scream at her that she shouldn't have died, but I can't. I promised Monica that I wouldn't be angry, and now I must honor my word. To steady myself, I take a deep breath, pulling air all the way into the deepest part of my gut, which is churning with a whirlpool of misery.

As always, I know there is one pursuit that can calm my nerves. I leave Monica's cello where it is and reach for my Speranza. She is my companion most constant. We are alone in the rehearsal hall, she and I, because I don't want to go to dinner.

I find a bench close to one of the big windows, and I seat myself so that I can look out at the water. I cradle my cello between my calves, and I raise my bow with my right hand. I close my eyes and feel the energy of grief swirling inside me. The strings vibrate under the touch of the bow, and I channel the force of grief through my arms into the music. Monica's death has unleashed in me an obsession, and I lose myself in a mysterious force when I play now.

Left hand changes chords, bow slides over strings, left hand changes chords, bow slides over strings—faster, faster, faster.

When I pause to turn the page, I hear Don Vivaldi clearing his throat behind me.

"Bravissima, Isabella dal Cello," he says, walking to stand in front of me. "You impress me. You played that movement very, very well."

"*Grazie,* Don Vivaldi," I reply. I appreciate his compliment, but I'm not playing this evening to impress him, or anybody else. I'm playing for Monica.

"This afternoon I heard Catherine practicing her oboe," he continues, "and she too is greatly improving."

I agree. Catherine sorely feels Monica's loss also. She frequently joins me here at odd hours and sits with her oboe, the long slender woodwind instrument, losing herself as she plays its haunting music.

"I wonder...," Don Vivaldi begins, but then pauses in thought. A curious look of wonder radiates his face. He lifts his right index finger and stabs the air while he hums a melody—up, up, down, down, up. Then he lifts his other hand and punctuates the air rhythmically—up, up, down, down, up.

"I have an idea," he proclaims, his face beaming a broad smile, "the perfect idea for cello and oboe!" He turns and lopes out of the rehearsal hall. For the first time since Monica's funeral, a smile touches my lips.

The next morning, Catherine is already in the rehearsal hall when I arrive.

"Did you skip morning prayers?" I ask.

"I did my praying here with my oboe," she replies. I retrieve Speranza and sit close to Catherine and begin warming up. She is playing something completely different, but the sounds blend together in a natural way, and we each fall into our pattern. Other girls arrive in the hall, and soon the space overflows with the intriguing sounds of many different instruments warming up.

A piece of music falls onto my stand, and another on Catherine's, before I realize someone has approached us.

It is our conductor. "Try this." Don Vivaldi says. "See how you sound playing together."

We sight-read his roughly scrawled notes before us, and the blend of my cello's tenor voice with that of her higher pitched oboe is unusually pleasant.

"Interesting," Don Vivaldi says, nodding his head. He eyes us both in a considering manner. "Very interesting. These are just some passages I jotted down last night, but there might be something here."

I think about the plans that were set aside when Monica became ill the night of the wedding. "Don Vivaldi, I'm not taking lessons with anyone now that Cecilia has left."

He lifts his chin and brushes his red hair behind his shoulders. He studies me. "That is right," he says. "You and I were going to start working together, sì?"

"Sì."

"Then we begin in the morning, right after prayers."

True to his word, the next morning I begin lessons with Don Vivaldi. He does not tolerate sloppiness in the least, and from that first morning, my skills advance under his demanding instruction. I work hard for him, earning his heightened approval. In the full orchestra, I sit in the principal cello chair now, an acknowledgement that I am the best cellist in our ensemble since our dear Cecilia has gone. In time, the rhythm of Sunday concerts and daily rehearsals helps dull the sharp edge of grief's pain, but I don't lose the aptitude that was forged in the pain of loss.

One month to the day after Monica's death, I go to the sanctuary to light a candle and offer up prayers for her. Not that she needs my prayers, I think. Of this, I have certain faith—that Monica will know in God's time His blessing of the reward of heaven. I also believe that any debt she might owe in purgatory she has already satisfied. But it makes me feel better to go into the cool dimness of the sanctuary in the late afternoon and think about her.

So on this day, I go in and kneel in the quiet and let my eyes rest on our beautiful statue of the *Pietá*. I thank God once again for the gift of being able to cradle Monica's head against my shoulder as she slipped from this life. And then another thought intrudes—a thought that has been suppressed for more than four weeks—a thought about my ambition. On the cold night after the fireworks when Catherine and I were confined in the church, my desire to play a concerto solo burned bright within me. Now the embers are stoked again as I sit in the sanctuary. I want to play the solo in a concerto. And now I'm good enough. I know it.

On most Sunday afternoons, a violinist is featured in a concerto at our public performance. Annamaria is the most frequently chosen, and I will admit that she's very good. It is no secret that Don Vivaldi favors the violin players. I think because he himself is a violin virtuoso. I guess it makes sense that when he imagines new music in his head, he would most often think of the strains of violin music. But I also know that right now, and I say this in a humble manner, I am one of the very best players in the whole orchestra. And Don Vivaldi will notice and reward excellence.

Before I leave the sanctuary, I light a votive candle for my own special intention. For the next two Sundays, Don Vivaldi makes a point after the concert to single out not only me, but Catherine as well, to compliment us on our outstanding contributions.

The yearning to perform a solo flames even higher.

I have a lesson with him on Monday, and I know that I please him. At the end of our time together, he leans back in his chair and runs a hand through his thick, long hair. He nods thoughtfully and gestures into the air. "I have been working on an idea, Isabella, but I'm not yet inspired with its true form."

I look at him blankly, and he grins. "I know you want a special piece of music. I see that ambition in you, but… it has not yet come to me."

He rises and surveys the room, then looks at me. "It will come, I assure you. Your special time will come, Isabella."

*Oh, patience,* I cry to myself after he leaves. My heart thudding with excitement, I put away Speranza and fairly dance down the staircase. *My time will come….my time will come.* Going down the steps, I visualize the day: I will come forward with Speranza, walking with the same kind of grace displayed by Cecilia, play my featured solo and all of Venice will be awed by Isabella dal Cello and her brilliant talent. Every day brings me one sunrise closer to my dream.

On Thursday, June 27th, our orchestra rehearses a new composition that will be performed on the coming Sunday. It is a violin concerto, but several of the passages feature a cello and oboe. As the principal cellist, I play one part, and as the only oboist, Catherine plays the other. After we play our passage through, Don Vivaldi stops us and makes us start over. We comply. We play it very well. However, he halts us and makes

159

us start over again. This pattern is repeated five times, and each time, in my opinion, our performance is close to flawless. He holds up his hands and stops us again. I study his face, looking for a clue as to what he is hoping for, when I see a light of excitement dawn in his eyes. He claps his hands enthusiastically and points at me with his right hand and at Catherine with his left hand.

"I have it now," he cries. "I know what I need!"

He hastens out of the room, but catches himself just beyond the doorway. He turns quickly and tells us we are dismissed. It's not the first time Don Vivaldi has exhibited erratic behavior, so most of us just shrug our shoulders. Catherine walks over close to me, still holding her oboe.

"Were we bad?" she asks, "Or were we good?" She has a puzzled smile.

A wonderful sense of anticipation creeps up my spine. "I think we were good," I answer, grinning broadly. "I think we were very good."

We do not see Don Vivaldi again that day. On Friday morning, Catherine and I make time before our midday meal to go up to the rehearsal hall. She wants us to work together on our duet. I feel that we are well prepared, but Catherine feels an additional responsibility because she is the only oboe in the orchestra. One of the other girls, Valeria, has started taking lessons from Catherine, but her progress on the oboe is slow.

Catherine and I are already in our places on Friday afternoon when the bells call us to rehearsal. Most of the girls are in place when Don Vivaldi enters the hall with a thick bundle of sheet music. Without a word, he points at me, then at Catherine, and then he holds up part of the bundle. Without explanation, he picks up the rehearsal where we left off yesterday. I know what he means; deep in my heart I know what is happening. I inhale on a note of excitement and exhale a calming breath. My lips spread into a silly, wonderful, uncontrollable smile, because I think that my time has come. But I discipline myself to play the piece at hand the best I can.

At rehearsal's end, Don Vivaldi motions Catherine and me to the front of the room and grins broadly at us. "So next week," he says, nodding his head, "next week the two of you will be ready to play a concerto, sì?"

My impulse to squeal is staunched by my sense of discipline, and I nod enthusiastically. "Sì, Don Vivaldi," I affirm. "Catherine and I are both playing the concerto?"

"It's a brilliant idea, isn't it? You both work well together, and I think you share your minds when you play. Each of you knows what the other is doing, and your instruments—well, each of your instruments blends and supports the other."

Catherine glances sideways at me. "We do play well together, Don Vivaldi. Thank you."

"Yes," I agree. "We'll put in lots of extra rehearsal time."

"I know you will," he says. "You already have. You have earned the honor. So now," he adds, giving us each a sheaf of music, "here are your parts. We will perform *Concerto for Cello and Oboe* a week from Sunday. We will begin rehearsals, of course, on Monday."

"*Grazie*, Don Vivaldi," I affirm. "We will make you proud."

Once again, he nods and looks at me. "I see a little of me in you," he says with a smile. "I know you will play your part in an excellent manner."

Later that night I am drawn to the church. My prayers have been answered; my dream is about to come true! Oh, others might have thought me just a silly girl to put such store in the goal of playing the solo in a concerto, but that desire has been my passion, the force driving me. True, I will share my dream—it will not be mine alone—but I have already altered my fantasy to include Catherine beside me, each of us wearing a lovely white concert dress, each of us wearing a vivid red pomegranate blossom.

Kneeling before the altar, I gaze upon Mother Mary holding Jesus. I try to compose a profound prayer to offer, but instead the joyous strains of "thank you, thank you, thank you" swell my heart. For some minutes I sit in contemplation and notice again Mary's loving devotion to her child.

An unwelcome vision nags at the corners of my mind before I leave the church—I can't help thinking about the possibility of my mother being in the concert crowd. Would she be proud of me? But then I shove the thought away—she abandoned me all those years ago. She didn't want me. My mother doesn't deserve to hear me play. I turn my thoughts instead to Catherine, and how we'll have to practice with intensity to be ready for our moment of glory, just a little over a week away.

We practice whenever we get the chance over the next few days. In spite of this honor, we're given no slack in our academic studies or in our chores. We are expected to keep up with the translations of Cicero and the calculations of mathematical mysteries that challenge most of us. But it is with great devotion and enthusiasm that Catherine and I race up to the rehearsal hall whenever we find the opportunity, eager to practice *Concerto for Cello and Oboe*. Vivaldi has written a beautiful piece for us, with music that perfectly balances the voices of the two instruments. Perhaps I am vain and arrogant, but I believe I am very good at my part. Catherine is also good at hers.

Late on Thursday afternoon Catherine and I rehearse with the full orchestra, and my contentment and satisfaction with life are almost complete.

"I wish the screen weren't there," I say to Catherine after we finish. "I wish that everyone in the sanctuary could see us when we play. I wish they could see us in our white dresses, with pomegranate blossoms tucked behind our ears." I know that with her taller carriage and striking white-gold hair, Catherine is more eye-catching than I, but I too will be pretty on the day of the concert.

"But we'll play so magnificently," says Catherine, "that the crowd will love us blindly and be generous with their donations."

"I hope so. Then Signora Priora will have to admit that we have some worth!"

Don Vivaldi approaches and nods with a smile. "Very good, my girls. You do make me proud, and I look forward to our concert on Sunday afternoon. The blend of the cello with the oboe is beautifully unique, and no two other instruments could produce this special kind of beauty that I heard at our rehearsal today!"

Before he leaves the hall, he spreads compliments all around the orchestra, leaving the girls in a good mood as they put away instruments and drift down the stairs to get ready for dinner. I need to catch my breath and wander over to the window. Catherine follows.

"You are very happy, *sì*?" asks Catherine. "I remember that you prayed for this that night we had to kneel in the church."

"Oh, happier than I could imagine!" I exclaim. "This is the best gift I have ever been given. I have prayed for it often. Don't you feel the same?"

She pauses for a moment, lost in thought. "*Sì*, I am happy, but I think this is your dream more than it is mine. But I want you to know what a good friend you are to share your dream with me."

I shrug. "I hope that on Sunday we'll be magnificent, but I hope that Don Vivaldi will choose me again to play a concerto, perhaps next time just my cello as a solo."

"The music he wrote for us is exceptionally beautiful, isn't it? Many of his pieces sound alike, but this one stands out, I think. He is right that he captured a special sound with the cello and the oboe."

I sigh with contentment and look out on the lagoon glistening in the light of the sinking sun. The days have lengthened with the arrival of summer. Small boats and gondolas bob in the water, and colorfully garbed people scurry by on the walk below. Across the *Canale di San Marco* stands the *campanile*, the bell tower, of San Giorgio Maggiore. I always think of Monica whenever I see it, but today her memory makes me smile. I know Monica would be so proud of me if she were here.

Beside me, Catherine cocks her head in curiosity. "Look," she says, pointing, "have we seen that ship before?"

I look in the direction she indicates and see the ship that is gliding like a swan into the lagoon. I study it for a moment, then recognize the English markings that are unique to it. "Yes," I answer. "I'm almost positive it is the very same ship that sailed by the day we were outside practicing for Cecilia's wedding."

Catherine claps her hands. "That's right! The sailors made us lose our focus because we were all waving back at them." She shakes her head and adds, "Signora Priora was so mad at us for that."

"Do you remember," I ask, "how even Monica started waving at them? Do you think it's odd the same ship is back already?"

"There you go again, looking for trouble," Catherine laughs. And then she shrugs. "Who knows? If we stood at the window all day, we'd probably see lots of ships returning. This is Venice, of course."

An unwelcome intuition slithers up my spine, and I abruptly turn away from the window. A vise of foreboding squeezes my shoulders. "It's time to go to vespers," I snap.

Catherine turns and looks at me oddly. "Fine," she agrees, but she glances over her shoulder one last time before moving away from the window. "I think it's going to dock right at the entrance to the *Piazza* San Marco, just like it did before. Hmmm, I wonder what kind of cargo it's bringing."

"It's nothing to us," I say, "nothing at all. Let's go."

During vespers I try to figure out why the ship's arrival has made me anxious. I keep remembering how I was standing on the *fondamenta* before Cecilia's wedding when that ship's boy ran up to Signora Priora and gave her some kind of note. This has nothing to do with me or Catherine, but supper drags interminably. My appetite is weak, and my stomach starts to cramp. I motion to Signora Silvia.

"Signora," I ask, "I'm sorry, but I'm not feeling well. Please may I be excused?"

"*Mia cara*," she says, lifting my chin and studying my face. "You are looking wan. I tell you to go upstairs and wash your face and climb into bed."

"Thank you, Signora."

She shakes her head and makes a clucking noise with her tongue against her teeth. "You are working too hard. Don

165

Vivaldi has told us all how especially beautiful this concerto is and how hard you have worked. He speaks as though this is his favorite work ever. You must get stronger. You go rest now."

And Signora Silvia hugs me very, very hard and strokes my back. I take my leave and climb the three flights of stairs to our dormitory. Just as I reach the landing on the third floor, a heavy knock sounds on the thick wood of the door that opens to the front of the building, the door that is seldom used, the door that brought Monica to us. An irresistible urge to stop grips me. I look below and hold my breath, waiting. The light outside has faded to dove grey, and the foyer below is now in shadow. The demanding knock sounds again. I have to exhale a couple of times before Signora Silvia reaches the door. She peers through the peephole, and satisfied, she withdraws from the deep folds of her full skirt the heavy iron ring of keys.

My breaths come faster now as Signora Silvia tries a couple of keys without success. The third key unfastens the lock, and I hold my breath again while she opens the door. She steps back and graciously motions the visitor into the entrance hall. The door remains open, and light filters into the space. From three flights above, it is difficult to judge height, but I see right away that it is a very tall woman who rushes into the foyer. With a gesture of impatience, she flicks the lightweight hood away from her face, and I am stunned to see a knot of pale silver-gold hair on top of her head. Then another person comes through the door—a tiny, wizened Chinese man with a long, ancient braid hanging down his back. Following these two is yet another man, one who has the air of a local resident. The woman gestures excitedly to this man and speaks in a foreign tongue that I do not understand, but I recognize it as English. In turn, he relays the words in our language to Signora Silvia. The best I can understand from my distance is that the group is expected here for a matter of serious business. Signora Silvia motions them to Signora Priora's office.

Then a fourth person strolls through the door—a broad-shouldered man with stately bearing who pauses upon entering and assesses his surroundings. His eyes sweep over the foyer and up the stairs. His gaze holds mine for a brief moment before he looks away and follows the others, closing the door to the office behind him.

My gut is squeezed in twisting pain as I shake my head and moan, "No, no, no," for I believe that a terrible reality is unfolding for me.

# Chapter Nineteen
## A Day of Miracles

I stand rooted to my spot on the landing waiting, just waiting with an inexplicable dread. My stomach seizes fiercely, and I hold one hand protectively over my gut while I clench the banister with the other hand. I see the action below as though I'm dreaming it, an unwelcome nightmare. The office door below bangs open, and Signora Silvia rushes from the room with a broad smile beaming on her face. She heads for the dining hall with an uncharacteristic speed. She's not running, but she's walking with an urgent light-hearted spring that doesn't match her large girth.

The foreign woman raises her voice below, shouting foreign exclamations that I don't recognize, and Signora Priora responds with calm murmurs. The large man steps confidently to the doorway. Once again he lets his eyes travel slowly over the foyer, down the hallway that Signora Silvia has followed, and up the stairway. This time, instead of ignoring my presence, his eyes lock on mine. I am gray with dread, and even though I know I'm being impertinent, I can't help staring at him. I swallow hard and absorb the fact that he stands below as one who is in charge, one who controls what happens around him. When I don't look away, he cocks his head ever so slightly in an unspoken question.

The sound of rushing feet breaks our stare, and I whip my head to see Signora Silvia emerging from the hallway, propelling Catherine along with her. The strong man forcefully puts out his arm to restrain the tall woman in the office, and Catherine is almost pushed by Signora Silvia into the room with the group. As the door is closed upon them, I hear—everyone hears—a shriek of joy emanating from the throat of the woman. Her cry echoes over and over again, seemingly from the very depths of her being, and doors and walls cannot contain her thrill of discovery as her words reverberate throughout our *Ospedale della Pietà*: "My Catherine, my Catherine, my Catherine...."

Stunned, I stumble from the landing and seek refuge in the rehearsal hall. I sit alone in the dark, stroking the solid wood of my cello, my Speranza, and admit to myself the apparent truth of what I've witnessed. Catherine was right all along. Her innocent—I thought ignorant—faith that her mother was still alive has proven true.

The natural sounds of our building fade to silence as the deep darkness falls beyond the tall windows overlooking the lagoon. The girls will be in their beds now, all except me, and probably Catherine. At some point I hear through the open window the noise of a group emerging onto the street, but I bury my head in my hands and cover my ears. Perhaps I am dozing, or maybe just in a stupor, when a plump arm enfolds me.

"*Mia cara*," Signora Silvia murmurs, "you shouldn't be here all alone."

I shake my head miserably. "I don't understand how this can be happening."

Even in the dark, I feel that she is smiling as she lowers herself into the chair next to mine. "It is a miracle," she says softly. "By all the Holy Saints, this is a day of miracles."

"Not for me," I murmur.

She squeezes my hand tenderly. "It will all take some getting used to, I understand. But we all want what is best for Catherine."

"And you know what that is?" I snap.

"Isabella," her voice rebukes me, "what are you thinking?"

"I am thinking that Catherine's mother left her here all those years ago, and now she has come back for her. Why would she come back now? Do you think Catherine will go with her?"

"This might best be sorted out in the light of day."

I shake my head. "I won't be able to sleep now."

"Okay, then, let me tell you what I know, but I'm not yet privy to all the facts, so keep that in mind."

"Please, please tell me what you know."

Signora Silvia settles comfortably into the seat before beginning. "You remember that I told you how odd the circumstances were when Catherine was brought to us. And you should remember that it wasn't her mother at all who came to our door. No, it was a family servant, the old Chinese man, who wanted to save the baby. Heavens, he was an old man then. He must be ancient by now, but he is getting around quite well."

"He was the one with them today?"

"Yes, the very same man. He was determined to lead Catherine's mother to the same door where he brought the baby."

"But did you tell me that her mother had died aboard the ship?" I ask, still trying to unravel the knots in my best friend's history.

"We thought so," she affirms. "But we were wrong. Catherine's mother—Signora Mills—told us her story through the translator this afternoon. I tell you, Isabella, there wasn't a dry eye in the room. Even the translator wept at Signora Mills' story."

I almost smile when I add, "No tears from Signora Priora, I bet."

"There you would be wrong, because even our dear prioress had a tear or two trickling down her cheek as the tale was revealed. You see, the sick young mother fought to live all those years ago. Two days back out to sea her fever broke, and she began to recover."

"But she didn't come back to get her baby," I accuse.

"She didn't know the truth of what had happened. Her servant was a good man and tried to do the right thing, but he didn't know how to correct his mistake. He was terrified. The ship was well on its way to England, so he told her the baby was lost in Venice."

"She thought the baby had died?" I ask.

"That is what she was led to believe. But here is the miracle on Signora Mills' side: she always felt she had a daughter out there somewhere. And, just as Catherine has always told us, she felt a connection to her mother."

I snort with cynicism. "Or so that woman says."

"No, Isabella, I believe it. She told us that she lit a votive candle every day for her lost baby girl and prayed for a miracle. The years went by, and Signora Mills married again—the big man who came with her today is her husband. He is part owner of the shipping company, a very important man, a very smart man."

"But why now?" I ask. "And how?" The explanation is still far too fragmented for me to understand.

"Because of the old servant," Signora Silvia replies. "He saw his mistress weep often, and the secret in his heart filled him with so much misery that he couldn't contain it any longer. He knows he is old and didn't want to take his secret to the grave. He decided to tell her the whole truth, although he fully believed she would have him beaten—or even killed—for doing what he did."

I think of the tall Englishwoman and how the old, stooped Chinese man followed so closely behind her, and I know that she could never bring harm to him. "And so they came at once?" I ask.

Signora Isabella thinks for a moment. "No, not immediately," she answers. "Signor Mills is a businessman at heart, very pragmatic, and he insisted that correspondence be sent first and the child's existence verified."

My left hand still supports my cello, but my right hand flies to my mouth as I have a flash of memory, the memory of the boy running up the walk calling in his accented voice that he had a message for Signora Priora.

"The letter that came the day we were rehearsing for Cecilia's wedding!" I exclaim.

Signora Silvia shakes her head. "I don't know."

"It must be," I say. Then the eventuality I fear forms itself into words: "And you believe that after we perform our concerto, Catherine will go with her mother?"

Once again Signora Silvia puts her arm around me and squeezes. "There are so many details to be settled, *mia cara*. Tomorrow in the light of day, everything will be clearer."

"But what about tonight? Where is Catherine now?"

"She has returned to the ship with them. But we will see them all again tomorrow."

I shake my head. "Catherine and her mother can't even talk to each other."

"They have the translator," Signora Silvia reminds me, "and quite frankly, Isabella, they do not need a lot of words now because they have each other."

173

I heave a sigh. "I believe it, but on the other hand, I can't believe it."

"It is all very confusing for you, I know, but you will come to understand what a wonderful miracle this is for your friend, and…" Signora Silvia halts.

"What?" I prompt her.

"What a blessed miracle this is for Signora Mills! For a mother to have her child returned to her must surely be the greatest gift Heaven could bestow."

Signora Silvia and I make our way carefully through the shadows of the room and descend the stairs, with my taking leave at my dormitory. Exhausted, I fall into bed next to Gabriella and have no energy remaining to contemplate miracles.

In the morning the dining hall is abuzz with the news of what has happened to Catherine. I chastised Catherine because I thought it a waste of time to dream of her mother. I never wasted my time entertaining a fantasy of a mother who would come back for me. I look around at all these girls giggling and eating their porridge and wonder how many of them are dreaming of a loving mother who will someday return.

The bells call the *figlie del coro* to rehearsal shortly after our meal, but Catherine isn't back yet. My performance at rehearsal is acceptable, but not noteworthy. I expect a rebuke from Don Vivaldi, but oddly, he hardly glances my way. He does, however, pay a lot of attention to Annamaria, the violin player.

*Where is Catherine?* Catherine and I sorely need to practice our concerto. There is no other oboist who can substitute for her. Even though Valeria has begun training recently on the instrument, she is barely proficient. Without Catherine, our rehearsal is limited to the few other numbers to be performed on

Sunday. Don Vivaldi declares us done for the day long before the scheduled end time. He rakes his fingers through his long red hair and snaps up the scores on his podium, then motions to Annamaria to follow him.

I remain in my chair, unsure what to do. Whenever Catherine comes to practice, I want to be here. I place the concerto music on the stand and start playing my part. I do not notice when Annamaria returns to the room, but when she stands before me, I pause.

"You are practicing your concerto solo," she says feebly.

I nod. "I don't want to fall behind. I want it to be perfect. I want to be perfect."

She tilts her head and barely parts her lips before closing them again. The silence grows awkward. I say, "You obviously played very well today. I noticed that Don Vivaldi kept giving you encouraging looks."

She bows her head. "It's not my fault," she murmurs.

Now it's my turn to cock my head. "What are you talking about? What's not your fault?"

She meets my eyes now, and the trepidation in her expression unnerves me to my core. I inhale deeply and set down my bow, then lay my Speranza gently on her side. "What is not your fault?" I repeat with a steely edge.

She swallows and blinks hard. "We are going to play a violin concerto this Sunday. I'll play the solo, the same one I played five weeks ago." Now her words speed up as though Annamaria feels it necessary to race through this explanation. "Don Vivaldi doesn't have time to write a fresh one, so he says we can play one I've done before. He says the crowd will be different, and even if some of the same patrons are here, they

175

won't care if they see me again. Even though I'll need to practice a lot..."

"Stop!" I yell. "Nothing you say is making any sense! We're playing *Concerto for Cello and Oboe* this Sunday. It's my turn."

She shakes her head. "No. Don Vivaldi says Catherine won't be here. No one else can play her part."

Involuntarily, my hands go to my face as my cheeks blaze with anger. "Don Vivaldi is wicked not to tell me that himself," I whisper. "You better not be lying to me."

She shakes her head. "I'm not lying, Isabella. And I am sorry—truly sorry. I know it's your turn."

As I think about what I've just said, I realize that I want Annamaria to be lying to me, because then it would mean that Catherine would be back, that we would play the concerto I so cherish in my heart and mind. But looking at the unmasked pity on Annamaria's face, I know that she's sincere. It would be easy for me to want to hate her because Annamaria has played any number of solos. She is, honestly speaking, a brilliant violinist, and Vivaldi's favorite. She turns and goes to get her instrument. Before she leaves the room, she pauses in the doorway and looks at me, sitting still as a statue in my chair. "He can write you another," she offers. "You are really good, Isabella, and he can write another concerto just for you."

I stare at her in silence, and she leaves the room. I cannot hate Annamaria. She is not the one who is killing my dream. But the hatred inside is filling my lungs, making me feel as though I will burst. When I hear the foreign accent of voices drifting up from the sidewalk below and into the open window, I know where to target my hate.

It is Catherine who has claimed her dream and is now stealing mine.

# Chapter Twenty
## *The Broken Bond*

How can she leave me? Am I not the one who has been here for her all these years? I resolve to find Catherine and put the question to her, but I don't have to go looking. Before I have the chance to leave the rehearsal hall, Catherine enters the door—and brings the woman who says she is her mother.

On shaky legs, I rise as the two approach me, and the resemblance of the two steals my breath. Catherine is not dressed like me in the maroon outfit of the *figlie del coro* today, but instead stands tall in a new blue gown that accents the hue of her shining eyes. And her wispy pale blonde hair is pulled into a knot on the top of her head. Likewise, the older woman, just a little taller, wears a deeper, darker blue that highlights the startling azure of her eyes. Her light golden hair also is caught up in a chignon, revealing a porcelain smooth ivory complexion.

I see, and I hate what I see.

"Isabella?" Catherine questions as she discerns the expression on my face. "What's wrong? Have you heard? This is my mother come for me!"

I clench my teeth and nod at Catherine...and then at the woman.

Appearing unsure, Catherine proceeds with etiquette. "Mother," she says the title in English and continues in our own language, "I want to present to you my best friend, Isabella dal Cello. Isabella, please meet my mother, Signora Mills."

I call on every reserve of training drilled into me and drop into a proper curtsy, dipping my head to Signora Mills. She smiles and nods in return. I have no smile to offer.

"She doesn't understand our language, but everyone understands friendship," Catherine says with false light-heartedness.

"Not everyone," I say with ice in my voice.

Signora Mills' attention wanders to the tall windows, and she gives Catherine's arm an affectionate squeeze before she walks over there.

"Isabella, what's wrong with you? Are you angry with me?"

"What's wrong with me? How can you ask that? I hear you are planning to leave!"

"Oh, Isabella, of course I will miss you very much, but this is my mother. She's come, just as I've always hoped."

"But Don Vivaldi thinks you won't be here to play the concerto with me. What about my hopes? There's no one else who can play it!" I spit the words at her.

Catherine shakes her head. "I tried, Isabella, truly I did. But Signor Mills, my new papa, says we must go today."

"Does he speak our language?"

"No, but I tried to make him understand through Signor Francisco, the one who talks between us. I told Signor Francisco about the concert on Sunday and how I must play, and he told my mother's husband, but he said the ship is already behind schedule and can't waste another day."

My shoulders slump. "Waste another day? For me it isn't a waste. For me it's everything, it's everything I've ever dreamed of."

Her eyes shine with unshed tears. "He won't change his mind. I've tried. I am so sorry."

178

I step forward and take her shoulders in my hands. "You choose to leave me, Catherine?" I whisper. "After everything?"

Her blue eyes bore into mine. "It is my mother," she whispers in return, "my true mother. I have no choice."

"You do have a choice."

She shakes her head slowly.

My body stiffens, and I step backwards from Catherine as Signora Mills walks toward us.

"Then I have no choice either. You are no longer my friend."

"Isabella, please don't say such a horrid thing!"

Not understanding the words, but recognizing the plea in Catherine's voice, her mother puts an arm around her shoulder. I stare at them.

"You must bid me farewell," Catherine says, choking up. "We may never see each other again."

I am unmoved by the tears streaming down her cheeks now. "I owe you nothing because you are betraying me. You are breaking our bond."

"Please wish me God's blessings," she bites off every word. "Now, before I have to go."

I look at her one last time—her blue eyes, her blonde hair, the anguish on her face, and then I turn my back on her.

Signora Mills coos words of comfort in her language. The stone hardness of my heart prevents me from turning around as they walk out the door. After some long moments, I sneak a glance around the room, only to see that I am the only one here now. In spite of today's warmth, it is the coldest alone I have ever known.

I creep closer to the window, but am careful not to be seen by anyone on the sidewalk below. Before too long I hear the main door of the *ospedale* open, and voices spill onto the *fondamenta* outside.

I drop my chin on my chest and let the sobs overtake me now as I discern Catherine's voice. "Goodbye, Signora Priora," she cries. "Goodbye, Signora Silvia."

"God bless you, child," says Signora Silvia. "God bless you all."

The big door is pulled shut with determined force, and I allow myself to peek out the window. I see their backs as they walk toward the *Piazza* San Marco—and their waiting ship. Catherine is nestled between her mother and Signor Mills, both of whom have their arms around her. Catherine, wearing the blue dress of one who does not live in the *Ospedale della Pietà*, never looks back. As though it is someone else's, my hand rises involuntarily to wave at the receding figure of the blonde-haired girl.

"Goodbye, Catherine," I whisper hoarsely. I look around the rehearsal room—at the crucifix on the plaster wall, the mottles in the floor, and Speranza lying on her side, and all of it feels foreign to me. For long moments, I stand paralyzed by the dark reality that is smothering me. At last, I direct my feet to walk, and I'm on my way out when I encounter Annamaria bringing in her violin.

She stops abruptly when she sees it's me, and her eyes rest on my flushed face.

"I really am sorry," she says. "For everything." I look at her and shrug. And then I start to walk away.

"Wait," she says, "where's Speranza? Did you forget her?"

"I don't care," I mumble dully. I make my way to the doorway that connects our *ospedale* to the balcony in the church, and I'm relieved to find the door unlocked. I pause in the choir gallery and let my eyes adjust to the dimness before going down the stairs into the sanctuary. I breathe deeply on the bottom step as the spicy aroma of incense greets me. I am drawn to our statue of the *Pietà*, the marble representation of Mother Mary holding Jesus after he was taken off the cross. My head tilts to the side as I study the way the sculptor gave such great detail to Mary's left hand holding her son's hand, as though her long fingers are counting his. The fingers of her right hand trace a line down the jaw of Jesus. She looks so sad. With my eyes boring into Mary's, I put my fingers up to the line of my jaw and stroke the skin. What would it have been like to know the touch of my mother? And what would it have been like if Monica had not died? And what would it have been like if Catherine had not betrayed and deserted me?

I sink to my knees on the hard marble floor as these questions spiral incessantly through my thoughts.

"What if..." I am asking myself when I hear the tap of footsteps approaching across the marble. I do not turn around.

"Isabella." The hushed mention of my name is a statement. It is Signora Priora. I turn my head and look at her over my shoulder.

"You have been kneeling for a long time," she says. "I have waited, but I can wait no longer."

"As you know, Signora, I can kneel here for hours." My tongue is loose. "Surely you can remember. You made me kneel here all night long." I remember the bond forged between me and Catherine the night of the fireworks, before she and I knelt here together through the long hours, pain gripping our muscles and frigid cold enveloping us. But today she broke the bond.

"Yes, Isabella, I remember everything. But you paid your penance—and then some." I continue to look at her, but I have nothing to say.

"I need your help," she says at last. "I have come to take you to the office with me. There are accounts to be factored, more than I can do alone, and I know you are good with numbers."

I blink hard at her statement that she needs my help.

"Cecilia used to help me on occasion, and she mentioned how good you were with numbers. Please rise now." She offers a hand. I briefly look back at Mary's hand, and I refuse Signora Priora's.

"I can get up alone."

"So be it." She withdraws her proffered hand and massages the temples of her forehead as she walks away. I rise on shaky legs and steady myself before following.

"You will not be playing the concerto tomorrow. Did Don Vivaldi tell you?" she asks.

I suck in my breath hard and bite out my response. "He did not. But someone else did."

She pauses and turns to face me. "I am sorry. He should have told you."

I open my mouth, but I cannot call forth any response.

"I do believe that I understand how you feel, Isabella," she continues.

I follow dumbly, resenting her suggestion that she can have any idea how I feel. When we finally reach her office, she provides an explanation of my mission.

"The board of governors is meeting on Monday. They get together once a month to review our expenses and make sure we are using our funds wisely. One of them will come shortly after lunch to pick up my reports of income and expenditures. I should have completed them by now, but as you know, I have been distracted by the arrival of Catherine's family."

*Distraction*— for me, the arrival of Catherine's family was much more than a distraction.

"Working on these numbers will help take your mind off what happened," she says, "and also you will help me to finish in time. And you will see in our list of income sources that Catherine's papa paid us a handsome sum so that she could take her oboe with her."

Now she looks at me as though waiting for a response. I glare at her. "Well, then, I guess Catherine has everything."

"I am sorry," she says. "But you will assist here?"

Does she think I can refuse? I barely nod my head. "I will do what I can."

She hunches over the desk and motions to a stack of receipts. "Now here is the problem," she says, raising a magnifying glass. She holds it over the scratchy numbers on one of the scraps of paper and moves it closer, then farther. "This reading glass no longer works!" She drops it in exasperation on the stack of paper, startling me because surely the magnifying glass is far too valuable to be so careless with it.

"See for yourself," she commands. I take the handle of the magnifying glass and weigh it in my fingers, then hold it over the numbers. When the glass is close to the numbers, they blur, but when I pull away a little, the numbers sharpen. I find that when I hold the glass a hand's width above the page, the numbers look perfect.

I look at Signora Priora in confusion as I hold the glass steady. "Look now, Signora. The numbers are sharp and clear."

She takes a deep breath and bends over the glass. She moves her head, adjusting its angle and distance. I notice her hands are clenched and her knuckles turn blotchy red. With her head close to mine, she squints, then opens her eyes widely. *Clack — clack — clack.* She bites her teeth together as I have heard her do before when she is angry. Holding my hand steady, I turn my eyes to her face, only inches away. I have never been this close to her, and I have never before seen that her eyes have a faint milky fog on them.

"Signora," I gasp, "your eyes!"

"Yes, my eyes."

"I will do what I can." I sigh and put down the magnifying glass.

She gathers the receipts together and hands me the neat stack. She explains that I will go through them and separate them into categories — amounts paid the butcher, the dairy farmer, the vintner, and others — and find the totals for each category and then calculate the sum of all.

I grasp sums and calculations quite easily, so this won't be difficult for me. It will just take some time to work through this pile of paper.

"The report will be needed when the governors meet Monday afternoon. I expect Signor De Luca to come for it after lunch that day. Now, you will need to go to rehearsal later today for tomorrow's concert, but I think you have a couple of hours until then. I will arrange for you to have time to complete the task on Monday morning."

I snort. "I don't want to go to rehearsal. I don't want to play for Annamaria's concerto tomorrow."

"Well," she responds, "that is not an acceptable response. You have been, and still remain, a very valuable musician. That has not changed with Catherine's departure."

"Signora," I begin, but she cuts me off by raising her hand.

"Isabella dal Cello, there is no argument here." She clears her throat. "And you will kindly come to the salon for the reception after the concert. The Morelli family...."

The sudden ringing of the *scaffetta* bell echoes through the foyer beyond the room, stealing her attention, and she turns away from me.

"Wait!" I call. "What about the Morellis?" But Signora Priora is already going to the basket to retrieve today's baby. Before I follow her, I take a moment to look around the small room and notice a row of leather journals, occasionally punctuated by wooden boxes, lining the shelves to the side of the desk. Wondering about the contents of the books and boxes, I go into the foyer. Signora Silvia is already there with Signora Priora, and they are examining between them a splotchy, mewling infant.

"Catherine has gone with her mother today, praise God," says Signora Silvia, "and already He has sent us a replacement. We need to get this one cleaned up. I think it is a healthy one."

"You may take it," says Signora Priora, releasing her hold.

Signora Silvia notices me in the hallway now. "Eh, Isabella," she says, "another babe for the *Pietà*. What do you think?"

I stand mute and keep my thoughts silent. I think that I have been betrayed and deserted by my best friend. I think that there is a plan afoot with the Morellis. I think the secret of my origins is stored in Signora Priora's office. And I think this poor baby, whose mother has just abandoned it to strangers, will need the help of many if it is to grow up and have a life. That is what I think.

185

# Chapter Twenty-One
## *Facing the Future*

Signora Priora finds me in the rehearsal hall the next day before the concert. "Isabella," she says, "I want to remind you that you are expected in the salon for the reception after the performance. I have asked Signora Marta to accompany you." Without waiting for an answer, she leaves. Obviously, I have no choice, just as I have no choice about playing today.

"Oh, Speranza," I whisper, "what does it all mean?" I don't want to be here today, and I don't want to see Annamaria flounce to the front of the orchestra and play her solo. I don't want to play my cello to back up her violin. And I do not want to go to the salon and make polite conversation with the Morellis and their son Niccolò.

Or do I? As we musicians file into the choir balcony of the church, I step up and steal a glance through the openings in the screen that hides us from the audience. My eyes go directly to the center of the second row and he is there! I see his dark brown hair curling over his ears and his heavy eyebrows pinched together as he scans the screen. I pull away and walk on shaky legs to my chair.

Six cellos play in the orchestra now; several girls are learning, but they haven't yet been admitted to the ensemble. Valeria, the younger oboist, is not yet admitted, so no oboist will play today. I heard Valeria practicing yesterday, and she still has a lot of progress to make before she earns a place here. We tune our instruments, and then Annamaria, because she is principal violinist, rises and plays the note of A. We are supposed to tune to her note, but I don't care.

Don Vivaldi strides to the front of the orchestra, and I clench Speranza's neck. Before, when he has stepped forward with his distinguished white wig and his conspicuous red director's suit, the sight of *Il Prete Rosso* has filled me with pride and anticipation. Today, however, I feel drained and flat. In another lifetime, I could've shared my feelings with Catherine, but I'll never be able to do that again. I am utterly alone.

I play my notes on Speranza, but there is no joy or excitement in my music today. When the time comes for Annamaria to rise for her solo, I bite my lip with frustration. She is radiant and self-assured as she looks at the *maestro* and nods her readiness. It should be me at the front of the orchestra, wearing a pomegranate blossom in my hair and being the focus of every ear.

When the performance is over, I can't escape before Don Vivaldi confronts me. "Isabella," he says. "This hasn't been an easy time for you. I could tell that your playing today did not meet your own high standards."

I look at his blue eyes and can't read them. "No, Sir," I respond.

"Well, we will have a lesson together soon, *sì*? We need to work on some things together."

No longer wanting to meet his eyes, I drop my head.

"You are sad, Isabella, because your friend is gone. But you can find in your sorrow the source of your passion, and that feeling can inspire your music. You will come for a lesson in the morning?"

I shake my head. "I cannot, Sir. Signora Priora says that I have to work in the office in the morning and help her with a task."

"I will speak with her then and arrange another time for you to come for your lesson. She will understand."

I raise my eyes to his once again. "No, Sir, I do not think she will understand."

He smiles gently. "Signora Priora is sometimes a difficult taskmaster, but I promise you that she understands much more about the orchestra than you know. She understands it quite well. Now, go on and have a good evening. I will find Signora Priora and talk with her." He pauses and then adds, "I have much to discuss with her."

As soon as he excuses me, Signora Marta rushes to me, eager to accompany me to the salon. She hands Speranza over to Gabriella to put away and then shocks me by pinching my cheeks!

"You need some color, Isabella dal Cello," she says with a giggle. "You are too pale today."

"Ouch!" I rub my cheeks. "Signora Marta, I don't think I will be good company at the reception today."

"Look at me, Isabella." Her tone turns serious. "I caution you to make yourself good company today. If you want choices for your future, you have the opportunity now to create them."

She takes my arm and we walk from the church balcony back into the second floor of the *ospedale*. As we descend the main staircase, she whispers, "Annamaria was fair today, but I really wanted to hear you play the solo. I know you would have been *eccellente!*"

Her kind words put a smile on my face as I enter the large light-filled room off the main foyer. Don Coradini materializes

189

and takes my hand. "Welcome, Isabella dal Cello. I have recently seen your good friend Cecilia, and she sends her greetings."

I curtsy. "*Buongiorno*, Don Coradini. How is Cecilia?"

He nods enthusiastically. "Marriage agrees with her. She is a happy young woman."

"Please tell her I say hello if you see her again. I miss her greatly."

"I will tell her. I expect that her husband will soon bring her to one of your concerts." He links my arm in his and guides me toward a small group of people. "And now there is someone here who wants to say hello to you."

Signora Marta falls behind, but I know she is watching me, keeping me safe. The knot of people, most of them holding glasses of wine, parts for Don Coradini, and then I am face to face with Niccolò Morelli's parents. Signora Morelli is reserved as she extends her hand and her greeting, and I very deliberately drop in a graceful curtsy. Her husband extends a jovial greeting, and I relax. As Signor Morelli's beefy hand is holding mine, Niccolò walks up next to him. His lips spread into a lazy grin, and he extends his hand.

"Signorina Isabella," he says, "it is a pleasure to see you again."

I feel a slow heat creeping up my neck as I look at his outstretched hand. I glance over my shoulder at Signora Marta, and she gives me an almost imperceptible nod. I accept his hand, and he holds it for a bare instant before releasing it.

"Thank you. It's nice to see you again, too," I say.

"We were hoping to hear you play the solo today." His mother's words surprise me. "It was quite the news to hear about the matter with that English girl."

I sputter and clear my throat. "Catherine—her name is, was, Catherine."

Signor Morelli folds his arms across his barrel chest. "My friend Coradini told us last week that you were scheduled to play the solo today, so we wanted to come. *Sì*, Niccolò?"

Niccolò nods. "We were glad that it wasn't you taken away on the English ship."

Now the slow heat creeps up my temples and through my scalp. I sense that Signora Marta has taken a step closer to me.

"We visited earlier with your prioress," says Signora Morelli, "and she reported that she is going to teach you to help with some accounting. You are good with numbers?"

I clear my throat. "In all humility, I can say that I do have some skill with figures and sums."

His mother smiles ever so slightly now. "There is no need to be restrained by your modesty, Signorina Isabella. I asked an honest question and desired an honest answer. But it is a very valuable talent to have, the skill to work with numbers." She bows her head deferentially. "I myself have that skill and talent."

Signor Morelli pats his wife on her shoulder. "I am very proud of the work she does. My wife keeps all the accounts for my business."

"And me, Father?" Niccolò asks playfully. "Am I not good with numbers too?"

Signor Morelli beams. "Yes, you are very good with numbers, too."

"But our son will one day have the responsibility for the whole business," says Signora, "and he will not have time for the task of accounting. Someone else trustworthy will be responsible."

I look at Niccolò, and I am not sure how to address him, so I don't call him anything. "What is the business of your family?"

The playful manner in Niccolò evaporates as he squares his shoulders and lifts his chin. "We are in the spice business," he proclaims. "For five generations the Morellis have been building good relationships with sellers and buyers, and they all know we deal with only the best cinnamon and cardamom."

"We are proud of our livelihood," his mother states with an approving nod. "But let us return to you, Isabella. Do you have any other talents and skills?"

I cock my head. "Well, I play the cello. I am the principal cellist."

"Oh, that," she says. "I mean other than that."

At a loss, I shift my gaze from one to the other of the Morellis. The gap of silence grows awkward until I rest my eyes on Niccolò. He smiles and gives me the slightest nod.

Encouraged, I try to think of something. "I can embroider a little, but beyond that my skills with a needle are not noteworthy. And I confess that I can play chess pretty well. I like strategy."

"Chess!" booms Signor Morelli. "A fine game."

"Strategy is certainly a worthy pursuit, especially when it is coupled with a head for numbers," says Signora Morelli.

"I like chess too," agrees Niccolò with an enthusiastic nod of his head. "It would be nice to have a new opponent. Perhaps…"

"Excuse me." Signora Priora interrupts us with her commanding presence. I will not know today what Niccolò intended to say.

"Welcome, Signora," says Signora Morelli. "We are having a nice chat with your Isabella dal Cello and learning more about her. Her skills appear admirable."

"We were speaking of that English girl earlier," says Signor Morelli in his big voice. "You are not keeping any secrets about Signorina Isabella, are you?" He slaps his thigh as though he has made an irresistible joke, and we all stare at him.

Unbidden, the specter of a foe hidden behind a black cat mask rises in my memory, and unease makes me sharply draw in my breath. Signor Morelli can't possibly know about my secret, but will Signora Priora safeguard it?

Niccolò breaks the momentary awkwardness by saying, "Father, she has just confessed her secret that she is good at playing chess. Perhaps no bishop is safe from her."

Serenely, Signora Priora adds, "Here in the *Ospedale della Pietà*, we live and work in the sight of God, and surely there are no secrets from Him."

They exchange a few more pleasantries, and I let my gaze return to Niccolò. I don't know for certain how old he is, but I guess that he's about three years older than I. He is tall, taller already than his father. I think that he thinks he is smart, and I find his confidence agreeable. When I look at him, I am unnerved by the feelings swirling in my chest.

"It is time now for us to depart," says Signora Priora, and she puts her hand on my left elbow. Before we can move, Niccolò steps close and takes my right hand in both of his. The heat of his touch bolts through me, and I flinch. He holds my hand too long, but surely it cannot be wrong, because he is right under the nose of Signora Priora.

"Goodbye, Signorina Isabella," he says. "We will meet again, *sì*?" His velvet brown eyes are soft.

"Surely, it is not for me to say," I respond, demurely nodding my head. He smiles at me.

His parents say goodbye and tell Signora Priora they will talk with her again. I turn away and leave the room, my head dizzy with bewilderment. Signora Marta is behind me going up the stairs to the dormitory. "You behaved yourself well, Isabella. What was it Cecilia used to call you? Did she call you *Piccola Gatta*? Yes, this afternoon I think you reminded me of a little cat."

I smile at Signora Marta. "Signora Morelli made me feel more like a farm animal she was inspecting."

"I think she found you worthy."

Signora Marta's words are still tumbling through my head when I try to fall asleep. Worthy—am I worthy? Five generations of Morellis have been in the spice trade, but I know nothing of my family.

The next morning, Signora Priora is waiting for me when I knock on her office door.

"Come in, Isabella dal Cello. Do not dawdle." I enter, and although I cannot honestly say she is smiling when she sees me, her face is pleasant. "I hope you rested well last night, for we have much to accomplish this morning." She rushes into a detailed explanation of how I am to separate the receipts, categorize them, and log all the numbers onto a journal ledger.

"You can do this?" she asks. "You have not asked many questions."

"You have been clear," I say. "I understand what you want. I will be done before lunch."

"Very well, and...um...I am curious. Did you enjoy yourself at the reception yesterday?"

194

I look at her, look right into her fog-blurred eyes. "Truly, Signora, I do not mean to be impertinent, but why do you ask?"

She looks back at me, directly at me, and answers, "You are a smart young woman, Isabella, so I think you know why I ask."

I pause. "It was not unpleasant meeting with the Morellis."

She nods, and I screw up the courage to voice my question. "Signora, your eyes—what is wrong? What do you see?"

"Oh," she heaves a sigh of frustration and shakes her head. "This is my cross to bear. These eyes see outlines and general shapes, but they can no longer distinguish detail. As you witnessed, the magnifying glass cannot help me anymore."

"Well, then," I say, and can think of nothing appropriate to add. After a painful silence, I turn to the work at hand. "I will get started now."

"Yes, and I would ask you something, Isabella. This is my cross to bear, and I have had to share this cross with you, but I would prefer that it not go any further."

I look at her and understand that she probably cannot discern the expression in my eyes. "As I said, I will get started now." My heart softens. "And I am sorry, Signora." I work through the stack of receipts, separating them, and bemoaning the fact that my eyes will be taxed by this project, for many of the figures are almost indecipherable. I am eager to look up when someone knocks on the door, but I quickly glance away when Don Vivaldi enters.

"*Buongiorno*, Signora Priora," he says. "*Buongiorno*, Isabella." Today he isn't wearing his powdered wig, and his long red hair is pulled into a tail at the back of his neck.

"Good morning, Don Vivaldi," I say, not meeting his eyes.

"I have talked with Signora, and you shall have your lesson with me tomorrow morning."

"Yes, Sir," I say quietly.

"Try to get in some good practice this afternoon, yes? And now, Signora Priora and I have a meeting to attend."

"Yes, a meeting," she repeats. "I am ready."

I am startled. "You are leaving me?"

"You seem to have this task well under control, and Don Vivaldi and I have some important work before us. I will ask Signora Silvia to check in on you. I will leave the door open."

They leave the office, and I am alone. Hunched over the desk until my stomach grumbles, I become tense. I stand to stretch my arms, and as I twist my head from side to side to relax my neck, I notice again the neat row of leather journals lined up on the shelves. Wooden boxes are interspersed between the books, and I remember what Signora Silvia told me that evening in the courtyard—that Signora Priora keeps records of all the babies' arrivals and keeps any personal effects that are with them. I walk to the shelves and gingerly hold out my fingers, tracing the edges of some of the journals ever so slightly. Am I here in one of these books?

And then I am startled by the sound of an oboe drifting down the stairwell. I've been hearing in the background the sounds of scales and études all morning, but I'm perplexed at the quality of the tone of this oboe. I step into the hallway and crane my neck looking up toward the fourth floor. I listen astutely. I sat near Valeria on Saturday in the rehearsal hall, and I never heard her play this well. Her improvement in two days' time is nothing short of a miracle!

# Chapter Twenty-Two
## *Lessons from Don Vivaldi*

After our midday meal, I am replacing the receipts in neat stacks and reviewing the sums I have entered in the ledger when Signora Priora returns. A rosy glow flushes her cheeks.

"Are you through?" she asks. "I expect Signor De Luca to arrive anytime now."

"Everything is ready. All the figures are here in this ledger."

"And did you find this work tedious?"

I contemplate her question for a moment. "No, Signora, it was like completing a puzzle." I pause to analyze how I felt as I was working through her lists of figures. "Numbers are like music notes — they fit together in an orderly pattern."

She laughs. I have never heard her laugh before. "They *should* fit together in an orderly pattern, but that does not always happen." She relaxes into a smile. "I think you have done a good job, Isabella. I thank you."

"You are welcome," I concede.

She asks me to review all the accounts and sums with her so that she will know them all, and she assures me that she will remember every detail.

"It is an odd gift that I have," she says. "Once I learn something, I never forget the detail. It is a gift that I am extraordinarily grateful for, especially now that my eyes... my eyes..."

Her words trail off, so I clear my throat and proceed to go through all the numbers with her. A knock on the side door brings our analysis to an end, and Signora Silvia ushers in Signor

De Luca, one of the members of our board of governors. I expect Signora Priora to ask me to leave, but instead she presents me to Signor De Luca and motions me to her side.

"Ah," he says, looking me up and down. "So this is Signorina Isabella dal Cello of whom I have heard."

"Pardon, Sir?" I ask.

He smiles broadly. "From my friend Morelli. I will say no more. Well, I will say no more about our talented Isabella, but I have much to say about this."

He waves in the air the sheaf of papers he carries. "Look at this, Signora. I think the dairyman is trying to cheat the *ospedale*. Tell me what you think of this proposal." He shoves the papers at her so that she has no choice but to take them. She holds them in front of her face.

"It is absurd, is it not?" Signor De Luca demands.

"This will require some evaluation," she says hesitantly.

"Bah!" he cries. "Is this not a marked increase over what was paid last month?"

I bow my head to our governor. "Excuse me, Sir, but Signora Priora has been teaching me to help with the accounts. Might I have a look? It might prove a good lesson for me."

"Certainly," he agrees, and Signora hands the papers to me, exhaling her relief. I scan the scratchy figures and nod my head.

"As Signora says, evaluation is always in order, but it is correct that this proposal calls for the *ospedale* to pay significantly more than last month."

"An outrage," he sputters. "The dairy farmer is the nephew of the wife of Signor Coradini, so I expect our meeting of the board this afternoon to be quite loud and lively. Well, give me your monthly report now, and I will be off to the meeting."

He takes the ledger from Signora and bows to her. "Thank you very much, Signora Priora. You have always been a very good steward of the *ospedale's* resources, and I appreciate your hard work. We all do."

Signora turns in my direction as she says, "This time I could not have done it without Isabella's help."

After the departure of Signor De Luca, she says quietly, "Isabella, I do owe you a deep debt of gratitude. As you can see, I am going to need assistance here. Would you like to continue to help with affairs in the office?"

"I think I would." A week ago I could not have imagined wanting to spend time here, but today I experienced a sense of calm and order within these book-lined walls.

"I would welcome your assistance, but I will need to discuss the matter with Don Vivaldi. I need to assure him that you will still have time for adequate practice."

I heave a sigh of bitterness. "That no longer matters."

"Perhaps today it does not, but in time, it will matter again. And I would ask that you remember, as I always do, that we must make decisions that are in the best interest of the *ospedale*."

I am recalling her words of several weeks ago that everything she does is for the whole, never for an individual, when we are interrupted by a knock on the door. At the bidding of Signora Priora, Signora Marta enters and hands her an envelope.

"A messenger just delivered this," she says.

"*Grazie*, Signora Marta," our prioress says, "you may carry on with your duties."

Signora Priora turns to face me, holding the sealed message. She rubs her thumb over the hardened wax. She breaks the seal and unfolds the paper. I watch her as she holds the paper in front of her face and squints. She sadly shakes her head.

"Signora," I offer, "may I?"

"Can I trust you with any secrets?" she asks with an edge of wry humor.

"You know mine," I say simply, and she hands me the letter.

"Dear Signora Priora," I begin reading, "My husband and I request to meet with you on this coming Friday, the twelfth day of July, regarding a matter of great importance..." I halt as my eyes leap ahead to the signature, and I feel the color draining from my face.

"Let me guess who it is from," says Signora. "Is it signed by Signora Morelli?"

I nod. "Signora Sebastian Morelli."

The sight of her bold signature with looping flourishes haunts me as I sit with Speranza later and try to run through some scales and practice exercises. I can't focus. Giving in to my distraction, I lay Speranza on her side and walk to the window. Outside it's a sunny day with glints of light dancing on the water. I look up the canal toward the *Piazza San Marco* and think of the English ship that moored there just a few days ago. Catherine in her blue dress, and with her oboe, got on the ship with the woman who said she was her mother. Catherine didn't have the eternal brand of the *Pietà* burned into her shoulder, so perhaps she was never meant to be one of us. If she had been one of us, I don't think she could have betrayed me and sailed away, stealing my dream as well.

I lean my forehead against the glass of the window and close my eyes. I imagine the thrill of putting the red pomegranate blossom in my hair and carrying Speranza to the front of the orchestra, the excitement coursing through my veins. I imagine playing brilliantly and Signora Marta and Signora Silvia beaming their pride from the edges of the balcony. Then I see in my mind a ghost of Catherine wearing a black cat's mask and taking away my Speranza. The unbidden thought jolts me, and my eyes spring open. My hand flies to my chest as my heartbeat races, and I take a couple of deep gulps of air. I look around the hall, but all remains normal. Annamaria is practicing her violin, and Gabriella, her cello. Valeria is entering the hall with her oboe. I relax and take one more sweeping look across the lagoon before I return to Speranza.

My attempts at further practice today will be fruitless, so I pick up Speranza and carry her to the storage room. As I position Speranza in her case, I hear an oboe. The tone is not smooth, and the rhythm is uneven. Before I start down the stairs, I peek into the rehearsal hall and listen to Valeria. She is back to her old way of playing.

Don Vivaldi intercepts me and asks me to come for my lesson with him in the morning directly after matins.

The next morning, before I leave the sanctuary, I take time to kneel before the statue of the *Pietà*, an action that has become part of my daily ritual. For several moments, I empty my mind, just breathing in and breathing out. I need to say something, but I can't fashion a worthy petition.

"Dear God," I whisper at last. "I don't know how to pray, but I am so alone." While still on my knees, I study Mary holding Jesus, and I wonder yet again what my mother's touch would have felt like. The lingering sadness slows my steps as I climb the stairs, and Don Vivaldi is waiting for me when I arrive with Speranza.

201

He taps his foot and motions me to sit down. He is sitting in the chair beside mine. "I have been waiting. Time is valuable," he admonishes me and directs me to play through my scales. My stomach twists itself in a knot. My fingers slip on the strings. The bow feels unbalanced in my right hand.

He shakes his head. "You are not trying. Take a deep breath and find your focus. Now, again." I inhale deeply, all the way to the pit of my gut. I put the bow to the strings and try again. The resulting noise is screechy.

"Isabella!" he says sharply. He rakes his fingers through his hair, loose today at his shoulders. I feel the color draining from my face as I look at him. I bite my lip so hard that I almost draw blood.

"Isabella." His tone softens.

I clench Speranza's neck and lower my head.

He sighs mightily and rises to place a hand on my shoulder. "Oh, Isabella, I'm sorry I snapped at you. Your life has been hard these last few weeks, hasn't it?"

He looks around and my eyes follow his gaze. We are isolated in the alcove Don Vivaldi uses for lessons, so no one else is close enough to hear us. He turns his chair to face mine, clasping his hands on his knees as he leans forward.

"Look at me, Isabella." I am threatened by sobs, but I look at him.

"Music is what saves us from the sadness. My life has been hard, but when I felt like turning to despair, I turned to my violin instead. For you, you turned to your cello—you call it Speranza?—when you became Monica's teacher. I saw how music brought the two of you together as sisters, and I think the music soothed Monica. Don't you agree?"

I nod, and a single tear slips down my cheek.

202

"Ever since I was a boy, I have been plagued by this breathing affliction that tightens my chest and smothers me." He taps his breastbone. "But I find that picking up my violin and playing loosens the bindings and helps me breathe again. You know that I am a priest, yes? I took my holy vows with every true intention of serving God through the priesthood, but I believe God had other plans for me. Almost every time I stepped onto the altar to serve Mass before a congregation, the affliction assailed me, and I would have to leave the altar. What does that mean, Isabella?"

I look at him dumbfounded. "I don't know what it means, Sir."

He grins and leans back in his chair, raking his fingers through his hair. "You are wondering why I am telling you this, but there is a point. God wants me to serve Him with my music. That is my deepest, truest calling. So what I want to ask you is this, Isabella—what do you think your deepest, truest calling is?"

He frames the question that has haunted me for several days now, and hearing the question put into words unleashes a steady stream of tears.

"I used to know what I wanted more than anything," I sniff, "but now I can't say."

"You've lost a great deal in the last few months. You were greatly saddened by Monica's death, but I want you to know that your friendship brought great joy to her life. And now you are aggrieved by Catherine's leaving, but this wound will heal."

I vigorously shake my head. "They've all left me," I stutter on a series of sobs.

He leans forward very close to my face. "Look around," he commands, motioning to the girls in the rehearsal hall beyond the alcove. "They haven't all left. Many are here, and more come every week. Who will be here for them as Cecilia was here for you?"

"Cecilia left."

"Yes, because she had the opportunity to get married. Cecilia was a very good musician, but she thought marriage was her true calling. Now consider that prospect, Isabella. Do you think you would ever like to get married?"

I gulp in air as my sobs start to relent. "Maybe, because if I got married, then I would belong to a real family."

"Ah, we all want to belong, don't we? Perhaps that is the desire God plants most deeply in us." He sits back and pats his thighs. "We will let Speranza rest today. We will resume our lessons later in the week."

He sees Signora Silvia in the rehearsal hall and motions her to come to us. With a smile beaming on her face, Signora Silvia crosses the space with her slow gait. When she sees my face, however, alarm besets her face. I stand.

"*Mia cara!*" she exclaims, wrapping me in a tight embrace. "What is wrong? Why the tears?"

I let myself slump against her softness, and I close my eyes as she strokes the back of my head. She makes soft cooing noises.

Don Vivaldi rises. "We will resume our lesson another time, Signora. This hasn't been a good week for our Isabella. I'm glad you are here for her."

Signora steps away so that she can take my face in both her hands. "Look at you," she says, and shakes her head with a clucking sound. "I will go with you to put away your Speranza, and then you and I will go sit together in our courtyard. We have some time before the bells call us again. It's a nice thought, isn't it, just to sit in the warmth together?"

It is a nice thought. She still has an arm around me as we leave the hall. I am carrying Speranza, and she holds my bow. While we are in the storage chamber, I hear it again—I hear the beautiful oboe!

"Signora, listen!" I exclaim. I put Speranza in her place and hurry back into the rehearsal hall. I look around while I hear the strains of an oboe playing a melody in a minor key. Valeria isn't here. No one here is playing an oboe.

Signora Silvia catches up with me, breathing heavy from her exertion. "Signora, do you hear it?" I stand still and listen to the music. I think it is coming from a chamber somewhere below us. "Signora, I don't think that can be Valeria. Who is it?"

"Oh, *mia cara*," she says with a shrug. "It is not I with the keen ear for music." She gives my shoulder a tender squeeze. "Perhaps Don Vivaldi has a new student that you will soon meet. But let us go now to the courtyard and give the matter no worry. I do not want to waste our sunshine."

If I had a real mother, I would want her to be as kind and soft as Signora Silvia.

# Chapter Twenty-Three
## *The Scaffetta's Gift*

The *scaffetta* bell clangs on Friday while I'm organizing and filing a stack of invoices in Signora Priora's office. I peek outside the door. Signora Priora has gone to another meeting, but Signora Silvia and Signora Marta reach the *scaffetta* at the same time and turn the handle of the disc, so that the basket revolves from the sidewalk into our entry hall. As they lift the bundle from the basket, the mysterious oboe music floats down the stairwell. I hurry to the bottom of the stairs and put my hand on the newel post. This cannot be Valeria that I am hearing.

"Holy Mary," cries Signora Marta. "This one is blue!"

"Help us, Isabella," commands Signora Silvia when she realizes I am near. "Clear the desk in the office."

I run in ahead of Signora Marta, who carries the baby, and scoop the piles of paper off the desk into my apron. Signora Marta lays the infant on the desk and loosens its swaddling. Signora Silvia lumbers in, breathing heavily.

I stand back in uncertainty as the women uncover a little wrinkled girl still chalky with birth matter. She does not cry.

"Breathe for her," cries Signora Marta, pulling two edges of the blanket together around the child. "I see nothing wrong with her, but she is not breathing!"

Signora Silvia bends over the desk and lifts her eyes quickly to the crucifix. "Jesus, help me," she implores, and then uses one finger to open the baby's mouth. She puts her face down to the child, and in a motion more gentle than I've ever seen before, she puts her own mouth over the little one's mouth and nose, and

Signora Silvia breathes. With gentle puffs, she blows into the baby—puffs and pauses, puffs and pauses.

"Holy Mary, pray for us," intones Signora Marta as she holds the wrap snugly around the baby. Remembering my presence, Signora Marta adds, "Go, Isabella. Go find the priest and Signora Priora. Hurry! And bring Signora Pellegrina too!"

I drop the papers that I'm still holding in my apron and run into the hallway, relieved to see Signora Priora coming down the stairs. "I heard the bell earlier," she says.

"They need you, Signora!" I yell. "I shall find the priest!" And then the most beautiful music rings forth from the office—the hearty bawl of a newborn, one wailing cry after another surging into the *Ospedale della Pietà*—the song of life. Signora Priora rushes past me.

I creep back toward the office and look in the door.

"Oh, Lucieta," says Signora Silvia, looking at Signora Priora, "thank God you are here. But I think this little one will be okay. She is breathing now."

Signora Marta sees me and tells me that I don't need to go find the priest after all. Signora Priora runs her fingers over the baby's face and feels the baby's chest beneath its blanket while Signora Marta tells her about the newborn's arrival. Our prioress smiles and declares, "I feel that this one is breathing strongly now. I too believe it will be okay."

"It's a girl," offers Signora Marta. "And there was a token hidden in the folds of the blanket." She lifts a pendant and holds it so that we can all see the silver piece hanging on the chain.

"Would you please make the journal entry?" asks Signora Priora. "And make sure you describe the necklace in detail and put it in the adjoining box. It might make a difference someday.

Describe her condition upon arrival and how she came back to life."

"I'll take her to the infirmary to get her cleaned up first," says Signora Marta. "And I'll ask Signora Pellegrina to look at her."

"No, wait," says Signora Silvia in a very quiet voice, hardly discernible in the midst of the full wails, "let us pray. Come, Isabella, come and join us."

I follow the lead of the women as they cross themselves and begin the Ave Maria. I join them in the Latin prayer. When the prayer is over, I look at the three standing over the screaming little girl, all looking at her with relief.

"This is special, isn't it?" I can't help but ask.

Signora Silvia nods. "We lose many, Isabella, but we rejoice for those who live."

"With all respect," I venture, "could we name her Silvia?"

They all turn their eyes from the baby to me while Signora Silvia shakes her head in protest. But Signora Priora nods appreciatively. "A worthy idea—Baby Silvia she will be."

Signora Silvia snuggles the baby and tries to soothe her. "I'll take her," she says, and Signora Silvia carries away her namesake, cooing over the infant's subsiding cries. The baby will be cleaned off, warmed up, and handed into the arms of a wet nurse, a woman who has extra milk in her breasts and can feed a baby not her own. According to the standard ritual here, Baby Silvia will be baptized tomorrow at our early morning Mass.

Remembering the request to record Baby Silvia's arrival, Signora Marta goes to the bookshelf and scans the row of leather journals there. Signora Priora steps up next to her, feels the spines, and withdraws a book bound in deep blue leather.

"They are lined up chronologically," she explains, "with this most recent one at the end of the row. I am able to record one year's arrivals in each volume."

Signora Marta points to one lone journal on the bottom shelf. "And that one?" she asks.

"Ah, that one—that one is where I have recorded the special arrivals."

Signora Marta looks at her with raised eyebrows.

"You would find the story of Monica's arrival entered in that volume," Signora Priora says, "as well as the story of Catherine's arrival all those years ago. And others as well, but not many."

Signora Marta and I look at one another. Signora Priora breaks our silence by adding, "Everything I do is for the good of the *ospedale*. I have not always been certain that the governors would make the same decision."

She dismisses Signora Marta, but I remain to gather up the papers strewn about the floor and get them into order once again. I spread stacks of receipts across the desk, work to rearrange them, and Signora compliments me on my job.

I clear my throat and pause at my task. "You have a question?" asks Signora.

"Yes," I admit. "Signora, you said that Catherine was in that book on the bottom shelf. Were you surprised when that woman came and said she was Catherine's mother?"

Even though Signora Silvia has told me Catherine's story, my mind still hungers for proof—real proof.

Signora Priora turns her face to me, and I look into her eyes that appear as though they are glazed with frost. "Isabella, that woman is her mother...and no, I was not surprised." She sighs and points to the volume on the bottom shelf. "Take it out," she says. "I want you to see it."

With curiosity, I withdraw the lone volume and set it on the desk on top of the receipts. "I told you that I hardly ever forget anything," she says. "The day that we were practicing the processional for Cecilia's wedding, I received a message from a little ship's boy."

"I remember that," I interject.

She nods. "It was from Signor Mills, the husband of Catherine's mother. He was inquiring about a girl child who might have been left here about twelve years ago. He did not want his wife's hopes to be raised, only to be dashed by disappointment that such a child did not exist." She folds her arms and looks upwards, studying the ceiling. "I began thinking about the exact words that I had entered in my special journal twelve years ago, and I wanted to see if I remembered correctly. When I got Signor Mills' message, I could still see enough to barely make out the words in the book." She points to it. "Open it, Isabella. Open it to about the third page in and read to me what you see."

With shaky fingers I turn the pages and stop when I see the heading "English Child." I hold my breath as I witness the record of our history, and Signora Priora clears her throat.

"I want you to read it out loud," she says.

I begin. "Ship's servant, Chinese, delivered child approximately two years old. Man says that she was aboard the English merchant vessel *Margaret* with her father, who was the captain, and her mother. Father died several days ago of the fever, and mother is delirious with the fever and near death. When she dies, there will be no one on the ship who can care for the child. Servant begged for the sake of his dying mistress that we accept the child. Her name is Catherine. Child babbles in English language and carries a silver rattle."

When I finish reading the entry, I shake my head.

"Notice my words," says Signora. "I wrote 'near death,' not dead. The woman survived the fever."

"Catherine always knew," I whisper. "She said she could feel her mother's presence in her heart."

"Yes, she always believed, didn't she? She expected a miracle, and it came to her. Her miracle sailed up the canal one sunny day."

"How could you be sure, Signora?"

"Look at the small boxes on my bookshelf," she says. "They hold evidence of a baby's origins. When Signora Mills came to me, I asked her what token might have been left with her child twelve years ago. She brightly exclaimed that Catherine would have had her favorite rattle, a silver one. I opened the box next to the journal, and there it lay on a soft cloth. When Signora Mills saw it, she almost fainted from happiness because it was the proof—proof for both of us."

"Proof," I whisper. And my head spins with the possibilities of what I might find hidden in this room. Might I find the proof of who I really am?

"Did you have any other concerns?" Signora asks.

"No," I lie, my eyes scanning the row of journals and boxes.

"Then we need to discuss an important issue," she says. "Please sit." She motions me to the carved chair in front of her desk, and she takes her usual place behind it. She puts her elbows on the desk, folds her fingers, and leans forward. A frisson of fear slithers up my spine. What now?

"I had hoped to delay this matter a bit longer," she begins, "but I am pressured to take care of it now."

"I don't know what I've done now, Signora. What matter?"

"Oh, nothing to blame you for," she assures me. "Quite the contrary."

I fidget and bite my lower lip.

"What do you think of Niccolò Morelli?"

I exhale a sigh of relief. "What do I think of Niccolò Morelli? I think he is...is...pleasant." As I answer, I imagine the sight of Niccolò with his deep brown eyes and chipped tooth. "Why?" I ask.

"His family finds you suitable and has offered a marriage contract for you, Isabella—a very good offer. And they want a response soon." She leans back and sighs. "So there it is. You are young, and I had hoped for more time."

"Must I decide...now?" I have entertained the fantasy of a marriage to Niccolò, but always in some far-off time.

Signora Priora nods. "I am afraid so. But let us consider what this opportunity would mean. You would have a good life as the younger Signora Morelli. I have observed Niccolò and his parents, and I have no reason to fear for your safety or well-being. Instead, you would one day help Niccolò run a prosperous and well-respected business. You would be a lady and command your own household. You might even be a social friend of Cecilia's. It is a prospect that many of your peers would envy."

"But my cello? My Speranza?"

She shakes her head. "Your cello, your Speranza as you call it, belongs to the *ospedale*. It is possible, of course, that the Morellis might obtain one for you, but I can make no promises at all."

"And if they did get me a cello?"

She sighs. "The rules of the institution are quite clear: you will be required to sign a contract upon marriage that you can never again perform in public. You could only play in a private parlor."

I tilt my head to the side. "Because...?"

She half smiles. "Because the *Ospedale* needs the income from visitors who are willing to pay to hear an exceptional musician. If visitors can hear former *ospedale* musicians elsewhere, why would they come here and make generous donations?"

I stare into her eyes that cannot stare back and contemplate the decision before me. "So this contract is good for the *ospedale*?"

"Very good."

"Then you will make me accept the proposal and marry Niccolò?"

Signora Priora sits back with a start. "What? No! You have misunderstood, Isabella."

"But you have said more than once that every decision you make is for the good of the *ospedale*."

She shakes her head. "But this decision is not mine. This is your decision alone, but you must be willing to live with the consequences. If you say no at this point, you might never again have the opportunity to marry."

"What if I stay?" I whisper.

"You will have a place here, a place to live and work for the rest of your life."

I shake my head. "I can't believe that this is for me to determine. How can I decide what to do?"

"Pray about it," she says simply. "Pray that God will give you direction and let you see where your passion lies. But you do not have much time. In a week's time, I will need an answer from you."

"What do you think?" I ask.

"I think that other girls have been in the very same position you find yourself in now. I know of one in particular who chose to stay and has never regretted it—not for one instant."

I see satisfaction radiating from her face. "It was you?" I ask. For the first time, I see her not only as our prioress, but as a woman—the woman that Signora Silvia called Lucieta.

# Chapter Twenty-Four
## *Uncommon Beauty*

If I say yes to the Morellis, then I will be a member of a real family. I have always yearned for a real family, but I am fourteen, maybe fifteen years old, and I'm not ready to commit my life to one path or another. Is this fair?

"What is on your mind, Isabella?" Don Vivaldi asks midway through my lesson. "Your mind is not on your cello today, so what is it?"

Oftentimes our music director is abrupt and hurried, as though a devil is chasing him, but today I feel that he really cares. I tell him about the dilemma upon which I teeter, and he listens.

He sits back, runs his fingers through his long hair, and ponders his words. "Why would you stay?" he asks at last. "Why would you stay here in the *ospedale* when you could be a grand lady with a houseful of servants?"

"Why? Well, b...b...because of my cello, my Speranza," I stutter.

"I will tell you," he asserts, leaning forward, "since Catherine has left, and I know her departure caused you grief, you have not played as well as you can. I hold hope that you will be on fire again for your cello, but you are not the musician you used to be."

I feel a red flush of humiliation creeping up my neck. My tongue is trapped in a painful vise of shame that he should speak to me in such a way.

"But, Isabella," he asserts, leaning forward and staring into my eyes, "I believe you can find that passion once again. I have put my faith in you that you will once again play with uncommon beauty."

"Thank you, Don Vivaldi," I whisper. "I will try."

"Do not offer me empty words, Isabella," he says softly. "I was honest with you today because you needed honesty. Now, rediscover the fire that I know is still banked in your soul. And then, then you can decide where you want to spend your life."

I rise with my Speranza, remembering the last rehearsal I had with Catherine when I played my best and her oboe was superb. "Truly, Don Vivaldi, I do appreciate your words." I turn and take a couple of steps before looking back at him. "I am curious about something. Who is playing the oboe? Is it you?"

He smiles and nods his head. "Oh! It will be revealed in time."

After I put away Speranza, I hurry to the church. I am due shortly in Signora Priora's office to help with accounting, but first I want to visit my place of refuge. As I descend the stairs from the choir balcony to the main sanctuary, I am bathed in a glow of ethereal light. The sun streams through the windows, casting ripples of luminescence throughout the church. Have I never before been here this time of day? I am awestruck when I kneel before the statue of the *Pietà* and see how the marble-veiled head of Mary and the upturned face of Jesus are suffused with radiance. Mary's fingers, though stone, caress her child's hand with a tenderness I have never known.

"Where was my mother?" I whisper. "Did she count my fingers?"

I close my fingers and bow my head. Several moments later, I hear a rustle of skirts. I turn and recognize from her girth that it is Signora Silvia slipping away. She had been watching me.

I cross myself and retreat to the *ospedale* with a firm measure of resolve—I will not leave until I know something about the woman who abandoned me.

"It is I, Isabella," I say, entering the office.

"Yes," Signora Priora answers, not raising her head. "I can tell it is you by your footfall. Next time you will not address me until I speak first."

"Yes, Signora. What would you have me do today?" As I ask, my eyes devour the rows of leather journals that keep the secrets of our origins.

"Isabella, I hear anxiety in your voice. Is something wrong?" She cocks her head.

I pull my eyes away from the journals. "I am worried about the decision I must make for you."

"A decision you must make for yourself, you mean—to become a lady or remain a musician. So, I understand your nervousness, but I do not want it to interfere with your work today. I need you to be accurate and make no mistakes with the tasks I give you."

If I thought to receive any softness from our prioress, I was mistaken. "I am ready to work," I state flatly.

Signora shows me the jumble of papers that she wants me to go through today. "I hope you do not mind working in here by yourself," she adds. "I have a meeting to attend."

My heart leaps, and I smile. "No, Signora, I don't mind being here by myself." I fight to keep my voice even so she will not suspect anything.

After she leaves, I sit at the desk for several moments and my shaky fingers sift through the receipts. My eyes steal to the journals, and I calculate. If a year's worth of entries are recorded in each volume, then which journal should I check? I rise and tiptoe to the door, and as I gently nudge it closed, I hear the sound—the mysterious haunting sound of the oboe that has no player. This time, though, I recognize the composition—it is the oboe music from my concerto! I must discover who is playing it, but if I leave to follow the sound, I will lose my chance to look in the journal. I peek out the door at the stairwell in the hall. I look back. I swallow hard and push the door shut. I turn back to the bookshelf. I place my index finger on the spine of the last book in the row and count backwards fourteen volumes.

I hold my breath as I withdraw a nutmeg-colored leather journal. I peek over my shoulder; all is well. I gently turn the pages and scan the entries. I see nothing about me, but I am not sure where to look because I know so little about how I came to be here. I look at the door and then replace this volume and withdraw another. I look at the door and start thumbing through this journal. And then the hinges creak and Signora Priora walks through the door. I sharply jump and drop the book. It thuds on the floor.

"What is going on?" she asks. "What did you drop?"

She can only make out my shape. She can't clearly see what I'm doing.

"Isabella dal Cello," she says, "please tell me what you are doing right now."

I bend to pick up the journal, and with a sigh, I hold it up in front of her face. A hard knot forms in my throat.

"What are you looking for?" she demands. "If you choose to remain here, you and I will have to find a measure of trust between us in our working partnership."

I gulp a couple of breaths, but I can't get out any words.

"Do you know the burden I feel every day?" she demands. "The welfare of hundreds of children, let me see, I believe at the last census it was exactly 772, is on my shoulders. The school fills their minds, but I have found that unless the belly is full first, nothing else really matters. This is a responsibility that you might choose to share. So tell me—what is it that you are sneaking around to find?"

"My mother," I utter weakly. "I am sneaking around to find evidence of my mother."

Signora crosses her arms and sighs in exasperation. "This is not a matter you have ever mentioned to me before. How long has this concern been on your mind?"

Nervous laughter erupts from my throat. "It has been on my mind always. Forever."

"The other girls do not seem to be bothered by such a worry."

"But I am me, Isabella," I whisper. "I am not the other girls."

She moves to the shelf, takes a deep breath, and puts fingers to her temples in concentration. She then touches the last volume in the row and counts backwards. When she gets to the blank space, she turns to me. "Give it to me," she says sharply.

I hold it out to her.

"This is not the right one. You were not looking in the right year."

She replaces it and removes the one before it.

"Let me think," she mutters, and strokes the leather binding.

She offers me the book and says, "Turn to the first part of the book. I am fairly certain it is January you seek."

With a trembling hand, I take it and start turning the pages. The first entry is headed Giovanna; the second entry, Paola. And then I come to my name, Isabella. My heart catches in my throat to see the letters of my name neatly written in the top left corner of the page. Beneath my name is inscribed the entry *Feast of the Epiphany, 1702.*

"Read it aloud," Signora Priora urges.

"Feast of the Epiphany, 1702," I breathe. "I came in January."

"The coldest time of the year, *sì*? Well, continue."

"Girl child, about eight months old, found warmly swaddled in the *scaffetta*. Infant is feverish and has raspy breathing." My words trail off, and I repeat them, "Infant is feverish and has raspy breathing." I look toward Signora Priora's face.

"You probably would have died if you had not been given over to our care. Note also that you were not abandoned as a newborn. Is there more?"

I continue, "A short note written in the mother's hand identifies the child simply as Isabella." I look up and put my right hand to my chest as a sob gurgles to my throat. "I am truly Isabella!" I cry. "It says my mother named me Isabella!"

"There will be something else," Signora says. "Turn the page."

I carefully turn the page, and I see the treasure I have longed for—the scrap of evidence I have wanted. I gently lay the book on the desk and take out the worn scrap of paper that is tucked between the pages. I can hardly breathe because I am holding all I know of my mother. The ink is faded, but I tenderly trace the letters written in simple penmanship, no flourish. "Here is my baby, I named her Isabella. She is sick, and so am I, and I do not have the means to care for her. I love her more than my own life, enough to give her life."

I take this piece of paper, hardly more than a shred, and I hold it up to my cheek. I close my eyes and feel the touch of the woman, or girl, who wrote these words. I draw it across my face to my lips and press a kiss upon it. Wordlessly, I sink into the chair. I am very careful not to crease the note as I sit and hold it and weep.

Signora Priora wearily rubs the bridge of her nose. She speaks in a murmur. "This is a common story, my child. I do not have the time or energy during the daylight hours to think about where all the babies come from. I tell myself it does not matter because regardless of their origins, they will all be hungry tomorrow. At night when I lie in my bed, I sometimes think of the things I have seen. I have walked outside in the predawn minutes when the gray light filters through the walkways, and I have seen a cloaked figure huddling in the alleyway, trying to keep out of sight. I look in the *scaffetta* and I see a tiny bundle there, rarely crying—the babies are often too hungry and weak even to cry. I pick up the infant, and from the corner of my eye, I see the cloaked figure slip from view—another mother who made sure her baby was safely discovered before she left."

Her hand pats me on the shoulder. "Does that sound like abandonment, Isabella...or does that sound like something else?"

Through shaky sobs, I whisper, "My mother loved me." I wipe a tear from my cheek and look to the door when I hear the rustling of skirts. Signora Silvia enters and rushes to me.

"What is wrong, *mia cara?*" She puts her hands on my wet cheeks and looks from me to Signora Priora. "Why is she crying?"

Signora Priora nods to me that I might answer the question. "I have found my mother in the book," I say, my voice steady now. "She loved me, and she gave me my name. It is all I ever wanted to know."

As Signora Silvia hugs me and presses a kiss to the top of my head, two names come to my mind—Speranza and Catherine. I know what I must do on behalf of each.

# Chapter Twenty-Five
## *The Great Sacrifice*

*15 July 1715*
*Dear Catherine,*

*I am very sorry for being so mean to you. I think I understand now why you had to leave me and go with your mother. I have found out that my own mother named me Isabella. She left me at the ospedale because I was about to die, and she could not care for me. She said she loved me, and I believe her. I think your mother must love you very much. I am very glad that you are a member now of a real family.*

*Do you remember how beautiful Cecilia's wedding was? I have heard that she is very happy. Well, you will not believe this, but I myself have received an offer of marriage! If I say yes, then I too will be part of a real family, but I cannot help but be worried about the prospect of leaving. I would not be allowed to take my Speranza with me. What would you tell me to do?*

*My friend, I know I wounded your feelings, and my heart hurts because I did so. I ask you to accept my apology, and if you do, my heart will feel your response even though we are far apart. I am humming our secret melody right now. Can you hear it in your imagination?*

*I remain your devoted friend and long for the time when you might return to the Ospedale della Pietà for a visit. I said I would not miss you, but I do, every day.*

*Your best friend,*
*Isabella dal Cello*

I need divine help to get this letter to England, so I find Gabriella and Valeria and Annamaria and ask them to come to our room.

"I need you to pray with me," I explain, "because it's very important that this letter gets to Catherine. She must know how sorry I am for the way I treated her when she was leaving."

We gather in a circle around the letter and cross ourselves in the name of The Father, Son and Holy Spirit. We then ask for intercessions from our Holy Mother and every other saint we can think of, fifty at least!

"But we should add one more," says Valeria. "Let us ask for assistance from Hermes, the Winged Messenger."

"He is not a saint!" says Gabriella. "He is a Greek god."

"I know that," retorts Valeria, "but I don't think it could hurt."

"But the inquisitor might come after us for invoking a false idol!" warns Gabriella.

"Then we will never tell anybody," interjects Annamaria with a roll of her eyes. "It will be our secret in this circle."

"I agree," I say. "Hermes, please join the Holy Saints in helping get this letter all the way to Catherine in England."

"Send it in care of Catherine's step-father," suggests Annamaria. "I think he's an important man in England, so someone will recognize his name."

Feeling very positive about my mission, I take the letter and go to the rehearsal hall. I cannot explain why, but I want to play my Speranza in the presence of the letter before it leaves. I take my cello and bow from the leather case and run my fingers over the smooth wood. I carry Speranza, my bow, and the letter to a chair that sits in a swath of sunlight coming in the tall window. I tighten and adjust the horsehair strings of the bow until the tension feels perfect to my touch.

Seated in the beam, I position my cello between my calves and take a deep breath. I tune Speranza and then warm up with a few scales. My eyes close, my breaths deepen, and the force of the music tightens around me and lifts me into a higher realm. The warmth infuses me with energy as I play, and I lose myself in pure joy as I rediscover my music. This is it! Speranza has always been a source of life within me. I think I know which choice Catherine would direct me to take. And my mother— would my mother be proud of me if she could hear me play? The bells chime the hour, but I do not relent. I play and I play until the sweat runs into my eyes. When weakness overtakes my right arm, I lower my bow and rest my cheek against the neck of Speranza.

"Brava!" comes a voice from behind me, and I turn to see Don Vivaldi. "You have found it!" he exclaims, punching the air with his fist. "I believe your zeal for your music has returned. I have not heard you sound like that since the last rehearsal you had with Catherine. I am pleased with you—very, very pleased with you."

"Thank you, Don Vivaldi," I say, picking up the letter. "But in a way, I was playing today with Catherine." I explain to him about the letter and how I must make sure it gets to England. I have given this careful thought, and I think our music director has the best chance of anyone to help me get it there.

"So, would you help me, Sir? I think you probably have acquaintances in the shipping business. Do you think you could find a ship bound for England?"

He beams at me. "I would be happy to help. I will take it tomorrow. But today? Today you look like a girl who has found peace in her heart. I think you look like a girl who has fire in her soul for her music!"

I grin and nod.

"So, I think," he says, "that you are a girl who is ready to play a concerto for all of Venice. *Sì*?"

My heart leaps in my throat, and I can do nothing but stare at him.

"Your silence means *yes*?" he asks.

"Yes," I whisper, gripping Speranza's neck with my left hand. "Yes, but how?"

"I told you once before that I had faith in you, and evidently my faith was not misplaced. Look in the library and find the sheet music for *Concerto for Cello and Oboe*. Practice your part, and in two days we will have a full rehearsal with all the orchestra."

"But the oboe...who?"

"I have a plan in place," he assures me. He takes my letter and turns to go.

"Don Vivaldi," I call before he has gone too far. He looks over his shoulder. "I have a question for you," I say. "I don't think you'll find it silly, but I want to ask, does your violin have a name?"

He turns back to me and laughs. "Of course!"

I look at him expectantly.

"But it lives in here," he says, tapping his heart. "It is mine alone."

With a deep sigh, I sit with my Speranza for some long minutes in silence as images flash in my head—Cecilia, Catherine, Monica...and a scared young mother leaving her sick baby. All these women helped me get here, helped me achieve my dream. Thinking of my hopes, I look toward the tall windows overlooking the lagoon and the world beyond. Only a few months ago I stood there with Catherine, and she asked me if the fireworks were worth the price. I said *yes* then, and I would still say *yes* today. Our punishment was to kneel all night long in the church, but we prayed for our dreams that night. And Catherine and I both received our miracles.

For the next two days, I practice fervently every moment I can. Signora Priora excuses me from my office work, but asks me to return as her assistant after the performance. She says I have done a very good job keeping track of the accounts. As I rehearse my music over and over, I can't help but be mystified by the oboe part—who will play it? On the morning of the full rehearsal, I think I hear the oboe in the distance while I am eating my morning meal, but I can't be sure. Valeria, however, is sitting across the table from me.

"Valeria," I ask, "who's giving you oboe lessons now that Catherine is gone?"

"Signora Pellegrina has been trying to help me."

"What? Signora Pellegrina plays the oboe?" Now the mystery is solved!

"Oh, no, not anymore," Valeria answers. "She used to be a very, very good oboist, but now that she's so old, she doesn't have enough breath to blow anymore. But she can still play violin, as you know."

"But you just said she gave you oboe lessons."

"She still knows the technique, so she is trying to teach me. But trust me," Valeria shakes her head, "she does not play well enough anymore to play oboe in the orchestra."

The mystery baffles me still.

ISABELLA'S LIBRETTO

Signora Silvia is waiting for me upstairs when I arrive in the instrument storage room to prepare to practice with the ensemble. "I am so happy for you, *mia cara*. You do not need luck today, but I wish you *buona fortuna* at your rehearsal anyway." She presses my cheeks between her thumbs and forefingers. "You are too pale. Do not be nervous."

With rosy cheeks, I go around the corner to the music hall, my eyes searching the room. Most of the girls are already seated and tuning their instruments. Signora Pellegrina is sitting with her violin. Only one chair has been pulled to the front of the orchestra, just to the side of the director's podium. One music stand is before the chair, and I wonder why there is no music stand for the oboist, who will not sit. Where is the oboist, and who is she?

Don Vivaldi is standing next to the wall talking with Signora Priora. I take my place in the front chair and arrange my music on the stand. I begin tuning Speranza. The cacophony behind me of the different instruments being played in different rhythms and different keys exhilarates me with a delicious anticipation, and my heart pounds in my chest. When the bells of the *ospedale* toll the hour, Don Vivaldi comes to the podium. A hush falls over the space. I look at him and cock my head with my unspoken question.

He nods at me, and his eyes dance with delight.

And then Signora Priora carries an oboe and strides toward me. *Signora Priora is the mystery oboist!* She is the one who will play *Concerto for Cello and Oboe* with me! Signora has the barest hint of a smile as she smoothes the embroidered edge of her white cap over her forehead and draws back her shoulders. She lifts her oboe in readiness and puts the reed in her mouth to moisten it. Her long, slender fingers begin moving over the

230

instrument as she seems to familiarize herself with its feel, and then she tests the tension of the keys beneath her fingers. Shocked, I force my attention to Don Vivaldi, and he raises his hands. When Signora appears ready, I nod to him. He makes eye contact with me, then cues the opening of *Concerto for Cello and Oboe*.

I stumble over my first few notes, but Signora Priora plays with confidence, and I soon feel as though I am playing with Catherine. My focus sharpens as the deeper, warmer notes of my cello intertwine with the higher notes of the oboe. Don Vivaldi takes us through the three movements of our concerto, stopping as necessary to improve a sound here or there. He is demanding in his insistence that every musician here should be perfect. When the bells toll the next hour, he lowers his arms, clasps his hands together, and offers the orchestra a big smile. He nods to me, and he nods to Signora Priora. He is pleased.

When Don Vivaldi steps away from his podium, Gabriella and Annamaria rush to tell me how good it was, how well I played, how beautiful the cello was with the oboe. When I am free, Signora Priora is gone. In the instrument storage room, all the younger women and girls are buzzing about our prioress playing the oboe. Signora Pellegrina, however, tells us that Signora Priora used to be an oboe virtuoso before she devoted herself to caring for the *ospedale*. She would have been Lucieta then, I think. As soon as I put away my cello, I hurry downstairs to her office.

I rush through the door, but I catch my tongue and wait.

"It is you, Isabella. You may come in."

"Signora, thank you! I did not know, I had no idea...."

She lifts her chin and squares her shoulders. "I think there is probably much you do not know. But in time you will learn."

231

"But how could you play?" I ask. "You cannot see music, can you?"

"I cannot. You will have to thank your champion, Don Vivaldi, for teaching me the music and bearing with me while I reacquainted myself with my instrument. It has been many years since I have played."

"But you did it for me?" I ask.

She shakes her head. "Absolutely not. Remember, I never do anything for the individual. Everything I do is for the whole. I think that the wonder of our playing together on Sunday will inspire very generous donations." Her lips spread into the biggest smile I have ever seen on her face. "Big donations that will benefit us all in the *ospedale*."

"Signora, do you think my presence here benefits the *ospedale*?"

She pauses, and then nods thoughtfully. "Absolutely. I have no doubt that your presence benefits the *ospedale*. Of course, I did not always believe it, but now I do."

I take a deep breath. "Then I am ready to make a decision about my future."

She raises her eyebrows.

"If I can keep my Speranza and play forever, I want to stay."

"You will always have a place here," she assures me. "I chose to leave the orchestra years ago, but you can stay in it as long as you have the musical talent to hold your place."

I sigh as I think about Niccolò Morelli and his big brown eyes. "You will tell the Morellis? And tell them how grateful I am for the opportunity they offered me?"

Her brows knit in concentration. "I will tell them," she says, "but it is a matter of greatest delicacy. The Morellis are a proud family, and they have been generous patrons to the *Pietà*. We must be careful that they do not take your rejection as—well—a rejection."

"Then perhaps I owe them my answer in person," I say.

"It would not be proper," Signora responds.

I bite my lip as an idea forms in my head. With carefully phrased argument, I persuade Signora to let me meet with the Morellis on Sunday before the concert.

***

When I go downstairs on Sunday afternoon to Signora Priora's office, I am nervous, but I think I look pretty. Because I am a featured performer today, I am allowed to wear one of the better dresses from the wardrobe, a white satin gown edged with Burano lace. It is cinched up tightly around my waist. Signora Marta insisted on doing my hair, and she has pinned it up so that the graceful lines of my neck are emphasized. I pull myself up to my full height and knock on the door.

"Come in Isabella dal Cello," calls Signora. "Please come in and see Signor and Signora Morelli and their son Niccolò."

I enter and sweep a reverent curtsy before them. When I look up into Niccolò's face, I am assaulted by a momentary twinge of doubt. He offers me a broad smile, exposing his chipped tooth, and I wonder how it came to be. Pleasantries are exchanged all the way around. My eyes meet his velvet brown eyes, and they shine with anticipation. Life with him would be pleasant, even joyful, but how could I know from our very brief acquaintance what the lasting character of his heart might be?

I clear my throat and look toward Signora Priora. She nods.

"I thank you all for the esteemed honor you have bestowed upon me and the *Pietà* with your proposal." I look at Niccolò, for I understand that his pride at this moment is very vulnerable.

"Niccolò, marriage to you would bring me immeasurable joy and respect." His full lips lift into a gentle smile. Signora Morelli exhales as if her anticipation has been satisfied. Signor Morelli nods approvingly and lays his hand on Niccolò's shoulder.

I gulp a deep breath before continuing. "But as much as my heart would lead me to the certain joy and fulfillment of marrying you, my soul directs me otherwise."

I glance beyond the Morellis at Signora Priora, and her face is suffused with pleased approval. From this day forward, I will share responsibility with this dear woman for the welfare of the *ospedale* and the girls who find life here.

"I would like to marry you, Niccolò, but I cannot. I believe that I have received a vocation from God, one that calls me to serve Him by staying here at the *ospedale*. If I were to follow my selfish quest for happiness and say yes to the certainty of a pleasant life ensured by your generous and kind family, then I would be defying the will of God." I shake my head. "I cannot do that."

My heart flutters as I wait for someone else to fill the silent void with a response. Nervous, I cast my eyes to the floor. I watch Niccolò shift his feet. His father's fine leather boots remain rock steady. Then, after what feels like an eternity, Signora Morelli's buoyant layers of skirt rustle, and she comes toward me. She gently lifts my chin with her elegantly bejeweled hand and touches each of her cheeks to each of mine.

"You have come to a noble and worthy decision, my child," she says. "You have made a great sacrifice today, but sometimes that is what God calls us to do."

"Yes, yes," I murmur, "a great sacrifice." And maybe it is, I think. Perhaps I had not remembered when deliberating my future how handsome Niccolò is.

Signora Morelli turns to our prioress, who wears a very satisfied look.

"You have done an exemplary job, Signora," says Niccolò's mother, "of instilling virtue and goodness in your girls here in the *Pietà*."

"Yes," affirms Signor Morelli. "Yes, well done!"

I then venture a look at Niccolò, and I will say in all honesty, that he does not look overly disappointed. He stands tall, his shoulders square, his dignity firmly intact, even enhanced, I think, because of his role in The Great Sacrifice I have just rendered. He reaches and takes my hands in both of his. "I wish you well, Isabella dal Cello."

"And I wish you well, Niccolò." As I look at him, I have the distinct feeling that it will not be long before the Morellis will be out shopping again.

"And I will pray for you," I add.

Signora Priora clears her throat and sends me a glance that is unmistakable in its message: *be quiet now.*

The family departs with the promise that they will be at the concert in an hour. Before I leave the office to go warm up, Signora reaches and takes my hand in a gesture foreign to her.

"You have made a good decision, Isabella. I know that I have never regretted mine."

# Chapter Twenty-Six
## *The Red Pomegranate Blossom*

A flurry of activity ensues around me as the girls make last-minute adjustments to their dresses and hair, but I stand stoically and try to breathe deeply. With my eyes shut, I seek my place of calm. My day has come. Today, for all of Venice, I will play a solo in one of Don Antonio Vivaldi's great concertos.

I inhale with a shallow gulp, then exhale deliberately, but my heartbeat accelerates. With eyes still shut, I run a hand comfortingly up and down the neck of my Speranza, but my fingers are beginning to shake.

"God help me," I pray silently, warding off an attack of nerves. Then I feel a tender touch on my arm, and open my eyes to see Cecilia.

"You have come!" I exclaim, throwing my free arm around my dear friend and former teacher. "Oh, thank you so much for coming!" I have not seen her since her wedding day, and she has grown even more beautiful since then, radiating contentment.

"I could not miss your performance today, *Piccola Gatta*," she exclaims. "This is your dream, your hope. I remember so fondly the day you confided in me that you wanted to be chosen for a concerto solo." She must feel me shaking, for she grasps my shoulders and her eyes bore into mine. "Calm down, now," she commands. "You are ready. You have trained well," and then a slow smile spreads over her face, "and you had an excellent teacher, even before Don Vivaldi."

I sigh heavily in relief that she is with me, giving me confidence, and I agree. "Yes, Cecilia, you were a wonderful teacher, and it means the world that you have come to see me today. I feel like today is a miracle."

She examines me critically. "It will be no miracle if you pass out," she declares. "You are bound too tightly. Turn around and let me redo your laces. You must breathe." And brooking no protest, she turns me around and nimbly loosens the ties at the back of my dress.

"Now it is a time for miracles, *Piccola Gatta*," says Cecilia with a solicitous grin. "It is almost time to go in the church. Here comes Signora Priora."

Our prioress walks to us with her characteristic stride, and nods to Cecilia, and then nods at me. Signora Silvia marshals the rest of the musicians into a line in the *ospedale* hallway and orders them to go into the church balcony. As they fall into place, she turns to me with a beaming expression. "I am so proud of you today, proud of both you and my dear friend Lucieta...er... Signora Priora, I mean." She holds up a basket. "I have been in the courtyard plucking the best blossoms from the pomegranate tree for the two of you."

Signora Priora—Lucieta—waves the offer away. "Not for me," she says. "This day is for Isabella. And I do not want to clutter my cap."

Signora Silvia nods. "As you wish. I will need help with this, Cecilia," she continues, reaching into the basket and withdrawing a vivid red pomegranate blossom. Signora Silvia and Cecilia cluck and fuss and pin the flower at the back of my head next to my chignon.

"Look at you," exclaims Signora Silvia. "You are beautiful, Isabella!"

And, indeed, I do feel beautiful—not just pretty, but really beautiful.

"Now, my student," says Cecilia, raising her own chin, "remember posture."

I straighten my spine, throw back my shoulders and take the steps into the choir balcony of our church, the *Chiesa of Santa Maria della Pietá*. I hear the strains of the musicians tuning their instruments as I reverently carry my Speranza and bow. I pause just behind the orchestra and let my eyes roam over the musicians seated behind the grille that hides us from the audience below. The screen, of course, reminds me of Monica, and I feel her with me today.

On impulse, I step up to the grille and peek down into the sanctuary. As promised, the Morellis are sitting in the audience, and behind them Cecilia is finding her place next to her husband. Before I have time to dwell on the future with Niccolò that I did not choose, my roving eyes land on our statue representing the *Pietá*—Mother Mary holding her lost son with infinite tenderness and mercy. My gaze locks on the mother's fingers stroking her child, and I offer up a dedication to the two souls who shaped my life immeasurably—first to Monica, the little sister of my heart, whose burned and scarred face could not mask her beautiful spirit, who in her special need helped me hear my calling. And to my mother—the mother who named me Isabella, the mother who loved me so much that she gave me up to this life of music rather than let me die in the cold.

And then, my heart whispers, "Thank you, God, for letting me be here today." Silence descends, and it is time to proceed to the front of the orchestra to sit at the side of the concertmaster.

Signora Priora follows closely and stands just behind my chair on the right. Don Antonio Vivaldi smiles warmly as we approach. He is magnificent in his white wig and scarlet livery, every bit *Il Prete Rosso* who draws visitors from all over Europe. I position my cello between my calves and ready my bow. Signora Priora lifts her oboe to her lips. I look at her and see that she is ready. I barely turn my head, give the briefest hint of a nod to Don Vivaldi, and he raises his hands.

Then, the music takes over. The high strains of the violins sound first, filling the sanctuary with waves of melody; then Signora Priora's haunting notes join in, then the warm, mellow strains of my cello. I feel the vibrations of the music in my soul, and the quick and lively notes transport me to the wonder of fireworks, with the lower voice of my cello heralding rockets launched into the heavens, and the higher notes of the oboe signaling the explosion of bright lights in the sky—dancing, twinkling, spiraling down to earth.

Throughout the first movement, our instruments talk with each other in an excited and joyful way, and the orchestra provides the background reminiscent of never-ending fireworks illuminating the night sky. The music makes me feel as though I am spinning around and around with Catherine, pointing up to the dazzling spectacle above. My cello and the oboe have a break, and the violins swell, undergirded by the gravity of the bass. Now the rhythm slows, and we ease into the final measures of the first movement. The excitement of the fireworks fades away.

We pause to catch our breaths, and when I discern that Signora Priora is ready, I give Don Vivaldi a subtle signal to begin the second movement. Now the melody turns from light and playful to dark and moody. I feel the music's timbre, know it deeply, because it takes me to the terror of being trapped by evil men. Speranza calls out for the oboe, and the oboe calls back. I feel as I play, the threat of the drunken man in the evil cat mask. Hauntingly, the rhythm accelerates, and Catherine and I are running, running, trying to escape the clutches of the evil one. The music carries us through the dark, stygian lanes of Venice where we seek safety. As the second movement draws to a close, the melody shifts to a feeling of hope. Catherine and I are safe.

My relief is palpable as I breathe before the last movement. Signora Priora has beads of sweat forming on her forehead beneath her prim white cap, and I feel moisture at the back of my neck. I wait a moment longer and then nod to our *maestro*. He raises his hands, and I focus completely as the composition returns us to a feeling of joy and excitement. I feel the heady wonder that I did the day we stood on top of the bell tower and surveyed the whole world spread before us.

The music lifts me to the balcony of the *campanile,* and I marvel at the seagulls winging across the blue sky, wispy white clouds behind them. I feel Monica's happiness next to me as I play, my fingers no longer belonging to me so much as they belong to my Speranza. The song of my cello fills my soul with exhilaration as it rides the harmony of the other instruments, like a gull riding the currents of the wind, cresting and dipping, louder and softer. The notes glide along the marble floor of the church and soar into the peak of the ceiling, swooping among the beams, skimming along the fresco on the ceiling, swelling within the sanctuary.

"Breathe, breathe," commands an inner force, and my breaths come more and more rapidly as the bow slides across the strings. Likewise, Signora Priora loses herself in her oboe, and our instruments take on a life of their own and lead us to the last satisfying, victorious note of our concerto. When I have played my last note, I drop my head in wonder and thanksgiving. Rivulets of sweat trickle down my back beneath the lacings of my dress, and I relax my arms. I gulp a few precious breaths and numbly raise my head. Signora Priora is watching me, an approving look on her face.

Don Vivaldi drops his hands, turns from the orchestra to the screen and bows gallantly. A boisterous noise erupts within the audience. The people below shuffle and stomp their feet, and they blow their noses like honking geese. I rise and bow deeply to the orchestra, careful not to get tripped up in the voluminous folds of my skirt. Signora Priora, flushed with her own pride of accomplishment, bows next to me. At this moment, she is once again Lucieta. After acknowledging our audience with a grateful nod, the audience that cannot see us for the screen, we carefully retreat to the rear of the orchestra. The flower at the back of my head has come loose, and I remove it from my hair.

Instead of the noise in the sanctuary subsiding, the cheers escalate with cries of "Bravissime! Bravissime!" The audience loves *Concerto for Cello and Oboe* and the musicians who perform it! Don Vivaldi motions us to return. We go to the front of the balcony. I carry the scarlet red pomegranate blossom and hold it in front of my pure white dress. Signora opens the gate within the grille so that we might bow for the audience. We stand at the railing in full view of the people below.

For me, time pauses so that I might treasure the miracle of this moment. The girls and women behind me, my family, tap their slippers on the floor, praising a job well done. To the far side of the loft stands Signora Silvia, wide-eyed with joy, holding her plump hands clasped in front of her face. Before me, the aristocrats in their wealthy trapping stand and wave their handkerchiefs. Niccolò wears a broad grin and enthusiastically nods his head. Cecilia touches the tips of her fingers to her lips and then points them to me. They are all cheering for us. We are just girls, just women of the *Ospedale della Pietà*, and they are cheering for us.

Lucieta turns fully to me then and surprises me with an embrace. As I look beyond her shoulder, my eyes are drawn once again to the marble representation of Jesus in his mother's arms. This, then, is my *libretto*, my little story—I too once had a mother who cradled me in her arms and loved me. She named me Isabella. I became Isabella dal Cello. It is who I am. It is who I choose to be…and who I choose to remain.

# Author's Note

*Isabella's Libretto* is fiction—Isabella, Catherine, Monica, Cecilia, and most of the other characters in the book were created entirely in my imagination. Their story, however, is inspired by and rooted in the real eighteenth-century *Ospedale della Pietà* in Venice, Italy, and its renowned all-female orchestra. Several years ago, I took a music appreciation class and learned with great astonishment about this place in Venice where abandoned baby girls could receive an excellent education and become accomplished musicians. Visitors, including royalty, came from all over Europe to see this remarkable ensemble.

Venice was a city where music flourished, and Antonio Vivaldi, composer of *The Four Seasons*, was probably the most famous director associated with the *Pietà*. He was a Catholic priest who was known as *Il Prete Rosso*, "The Red Priest." I have presented Vivaldi in a manner consistent with what I learned— he was a temperamental genius, but he was also a sensitive soul who respected the girls and women of the *Pietà* and wanted the best for them.

This footnote of music history gripped my curiosity and wouldn't let go. I researched, read, and was fortunate enough to make two trips to Venice in my quest to learn more about the *Ospedale della Pietà*. With fascinated horror, I learned how the babies were branded on their left shoulders with the "P" for the *Pietà*, and I read with interest how the girls were often given a surname to match their instrument or vocal range. The records include mention of a "Susana dal Violin" and a "Paulina dal Tenor," among others. I also learned that the audiences in Venice

245

at this time did not applaud, but expressed their hearty approval through shuffling their feet or blowing their noses.

I had the pleasure of spending a beautiful spring afternoon in Venice in the company of Micky White, a British researcher and author who delights in her work of translating and studying eighteenth-century documents about Antonio Vivaldi and the *Ospedale della Pietà*. Micky mentioned in our conversation that no child was turned away from shelter in the *Pietà*, and my mind latched onto this idea and began to make some connections.

The prioress, or Signora Priora as she was called, was accountable to the board of governors who ruled the *Ospedale della Pietà*. The prioress kept meticulous records of the children who were taken in, and you can see some of these journals today at the *Piccolo Museo della Pietà* in Venice. But what if a prioress also kept a secret journal—a journal to document the girls who didn't quite fit the guidelines imposed by the governors? Upon this premise I built my story.

As far as Isabella's *Concerto for Cello and Oboe*, this composition exists only in the pages of this book. However, Vivaldi compositions were scattered across Europe during and after his lifetime, and miraculous rediscoveries of his music are still being made. As recently as 2010, a lost Vivaldi flute concerto was found in Scotland. Perhaps one day we'll read of a new discovery of a Vivaldi concerto written for cello and oboe, a concerto created by this prolific composer for two of the remarkably talented young musicians at the *Ospedale della Pietà*—two girls who dreamed of wearing red pomegranate blossoms in their hair and playing for all of Venice.

# Gratitude

Recently I heard someone note that if you break the word *encourage* into its parts, it means "to pour courage into." I smile as I think about all the people who have "poured courage into" me as I've worked on *Isabella's Libretto*, and I offer heartfelt gratitude to them all.

First, I thank my husband, Clay, for his loving patience (lots of patience!) and boundless support; and I thank my children—Caitlin, Sean, and Claire—for their wit, suggestions, and nudges to get back to work and finish the story. Their musical talent led me to discover the *Ospedale della Pietà*.

Thank you to the women of my three books clubs—the Governor's Square group in Charlotte, North Carolina; the Nashville book club; and the Aquinas book club. Sharing our lives through reading books together has enriched my life immensely and instilled in me a deeper appreciation for the power of the written word.

Thank you to the early readers of *Isabella's Libretto* who offered carefully considered feedback: Judy Rehder, Cindy Swafford, Janet Naff, Liz Meyer, and Maria Koshute. Each of you left a mark on this story.

I am not a musician, so I am especially grateful to Dr. Emily Hanna Crane, Coordinator of Orchestral Strings and Associate Professor of Music (violin and viola) at Austin Peay State University in Clarksville, Tennessee. In addition to giving me a violin lesson, Dr. Crane read my manuscript and patiently answered many questions. Any errors remaining in the story are mine alone.

*Grazie* to Annagrazia Vivetti, who graciously read my manuscript and suggested corrections to Italian phrases and words where she found errors in usage. Again, any mistakes that remain are mine alone.

I am grateful to the many friends I've made through SCBWI-Midsouth and The Writer's Loft at Middle Tennessee State University. The community of writers displays extraordinary generosity of spirit and willingness to help a novice. Thank you for pulling me along!

With a huge grin, I offer thanks to my dedicated critique partners, Cat York and Karin Blythe—the most enthusiastic cheerleaders anyone could hope to have! And a very special note of gratitude goes out to my youngest critique partner, Charlotte York, who is an oboist in the band and strings program at J.T. Moore Middle School in Nashville.

Special thanks to Linda Busby Parker, my publisher and keen-eyed editor. Working with Linda is a joy, and I am proud to share *Isabella's Libretto* with her. I believe this is a collaboration that was meant to be.

Last, I offer my deepest gratitude to God for the countless blessings showered upon me, especially the many graces delivered through the people who have "poured courage" into me as I wrote *Isabella's Libretto. Grazie Mille* to you all!

CPSIA information can be obtained at www.ICGtesting.com
Printed in the USA
BVOW04s1822151214

379496BV00003B/104/P